THE IMPORTANCE OF BEING
WILDE AT HEART

Also by R. Zamora Linmark

Leche

Rolling the R's

The Evolution of a Sigh

Drive-By Vigils

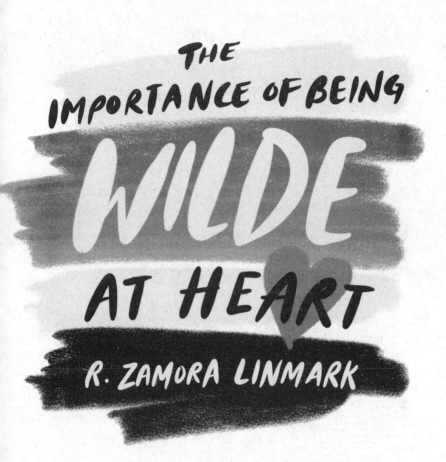

THE
IMPORTANCE OF BEING
WILDE
AT HEART

R. ZAMORA LINMARK

Delacorte Press

Text copyright © 2019 by R. Zamora Linmark
Jacket art copyright © 2019 by Connie Gabbert
Jacket photograph used under license from Shutterstock.com

Visit us on the Web! GetUnderlined.com

Educators and librarians, for a variety of teaching tools, visit us at RHTeachersLibrarians.com

Library of Congress Cataloging-in-Publication Data is available upon request.
ISBN 978-1-101-93821-8 (trade) — ISBN 978-1-101-93823-2 (lib. bdg.) —
ISBN 978-1-101-93822-5 (ebook)

The text of this book is set in 11-point Apollo.
Interior design by Trish Parcell

Printed in the United States of America
10 9 8 7 6 5 4 3 2 1
First Edition

Random House Children's Books
supports the First Amendment and celebrates the right to read.

For my mother, Cecilia,
and my sister, Maria Angelina

THE BOOK
OF RANDOM SPLENDOR

There are two ways to begin this story.

a haiku

LITTLE MIRACLES

Inside a minute—
A blue-throated hummingbird's
One thousand heartbeats.

OR

a prayer

Dear Oscar Wilde,
Patron Saint of Rebels and Bookworms:

This is Ken Z. I'm seventeen years old, a senior at
South Kristol High. I live on an island in the middle of
Nowhere, Pacific Ocean. So tiny you need a magnifying
glass to spot us on the map.

    Oscar, I met someone. There. It's out. Whew. Yes,
I met someone earlier this week, and this morning, I
woke up to my heart beating a thousand hummingbird
heartbeats. It felt new and strange, and anything new
and strange to me is worth exploring, like Antarctica.
I don't know where my heart is zooming to. So if you
could, please guide me through this unfamiliar map.

        Your forever devotee,
        Ken Z

PS His name is Ran.

How I Met Ran

Saturday, 2 March

I met Ran at Buddha's Joint, an organic restaurant for people who can afford to eat healthfully. It's located inside Mirage, an uppity mall in the newly developed community in the eastern-most part of South Kristol where corrupt politicians, celebrities, and foreign investors reside.

Worse, it took an eternity and a half to get there because there is only one bus in South Kristol that goes to Mirage—and it's the number eight. I don't even know why it's numbered eight because there isn't a one, two, three, four, five, six, or seven bus, unless they once operated a hundred years ago when South and North Kristol were still one nation. Sometimes we'll see a second number eight bus circling the island. That only happens during election, and only if the current leader is seeking reelection. We're very Turd World that way.

The actual trip takes only forty minutes. But if you miss, best to have an alternate plan or be prepared to waste your youth waiting for the number eight. That's why I always bring a book whenever I have to catch the bus, usually to go visit my friend

9

CaZZ, who lives on the Pula reservation on the west side. Otherwise, I walk.

I always carry a book wherever I go anyway. It's a habit I can't—and will never—kick. My mother said I've been doing it from age four, when I learned how to read. Nothing kills time more effectively—and with more fun—than reading.

This morning, my travel companion was *The Importance of Being Earnest,* a play by my favorite writer, Oscar Wilde, who is considered one of the best dramatists of the nineteenth century. It was he who inspired me to go bunburying. That means having a secret identity, an alter ego, like a superhero, except with bunburying the world is not in danger and there's no lover or stranger to save.

Bunburying is all about escape. Escape from your world, work, family, friends, enemies. And most of all, from yourself, from who and what you're supposed to be.

Everyone I know has boycotted the mall since it opened last November, right before Thanksgiving. They were turned away because they didn't comply with the dress code that no one knew existed until they got there. NO BEACHWEAR, read the sign posted at the entrance. NO SHORTS, NO TANK TOPS, NO SLIPPERS. In other words: NO LOCALS.

This, ironically, made Mirage the ideal place for bunburying. It was the closest to a foreign country I could go to without leaving South Kristol, and no one from my world would recognize me there.

As a bunburyist, I could create a fictional version of me. Or a version to add to the growing list of ME. For a couple of hours I could be whoever and whatever I wanted to be. No mom. No Estelle and CaZZ. Just me, Ken Z:

Adventure seeker.

Lover of spontaneity.

A daredevil who, for the first time, is leaving his comfort zone.

So, this morning, I put on the same outfit that I wore for Career Day, minus the brown-and-orange-striped tie that would've been perfect if I were trying to pass for a son of a Jehovah's Witness preacher. I even gelled my hair, slicked it back for the occasion, in case Mirage also had a strict hair code. I was all set, ready to hit the mall as an Aspiring Cultural Anthropologist disguised as an avid shopper on a tight budget.

At the main entrance, I breezed through the revolving door without a problem. The guards greeted me as if I shopped there regularly. At ten in the morning, the mall was already teeming with shoppers.

The mall's interior was grand: marbled floors, glass elevators, and the longest and most terrifying-looking escalator I'd ever seen. From the basement, where the food court was, the escalator climbed all the way to the fifth floor, where the medical and dental facilities were. I couldn't look at it without getting acrophobic.

Wherever I went, people eyed me up and down. Did I stand out too much? Was I that obvious? Did they know I was trying to pass for one of them?

I tried not to be too self-conscious. It was hard. I was not accustomed to getting so much attention. Best friends and mothers don't count.

Two teenagers, a boy and a girl, smiled at me. The boy whispered something to the girl; then they covered their mouths, giggling. They wanted to let me know they were talking about me. *Let them,* I told myself, remembering one of the immortal sayings of Oscar Wilde: *There is only one thing worse than being talked about, and that is not being talked about.*

The salesclerks were friendly, not snooty as I expected. They greeted me warmly, complimented me on my hair, my clothes. They treated me as if I had been born with a silver spoon in my mouth, a politician's or a banker's son, one of South Kristol's 1 percent.

Whether they were being superficial or genuine, I thanked them. After all, it was part of their job—to be nice, to make me feel good in exchange for sales commission.

In one of the shops specializing in men's formal wear, a salesman old enough to be a grandfather talked me into trying on a charcoal-gray suit. I'd never worn a suit before.

Inside the dressing room with its three-way mirror, I came face to face with a stranger egging me on to smile. From every angle, the mirrors reflected possibilities of me. A ME who stood tall and confident like a tower. Another ME who turned heads whenever he walked into a room. And a ME with thick black hair and intense brown eyes who was not afraid to look at himself in the mirror and didn't need to shy away whenever someone tossed him a compliment.

I smiled. If I must say, I looked good in the suit. But I could never afford it. Besides, it was all an act with an expiration time, like the midnight hour in a fairy tale.

By noon, bunburying had exhausted me. I was ready to bid adieu to my adventure, mess up my hair, and go back to my neighborhood with its horizon of clotheslines and cable TV antennae and crowing roosters and nauseating stench of diesel fumes and heaps of trash burning in backyards. And hang my bunburying clothes back in the closet.

Aside from false and genuine compliments, bunburying made me hungry and inspired me to write a haiku:

A pack of ramen—
Everyday diet for an
Anthropologist.

Famished, I went hunting for a restaurant within my budget. I ended up in Buddha's Joint. It turned out to be an overrated, overpriced, organic junkie of a joint.

I ordered the chicken wrap and kale shake. Two yakuza thumbs down.

Don't get me wrong. I'm not a picky eater; my tummy digests anything it can afford. But insecticide-free greens and grass-fed animals are too expensive for my taste. Chewing them is difficult. I also feel guilty eating a chicken that, while alive, was almost free as a bird. The kale shake sucks too.

Anyway, I was so engrossed reading the first act of Oscar Wilde's play about a pair of professional bunburyists that I didn't realize someone had been standing in front of me until he finally exhaled an "ahem." I looked up and saw a guy my age smiling and pointing to the sign taped on the Formica table. SHARE THE SEAT OF COMPASSION AND WIN A FRIEND.

I nearly fell off my chair. I thought my mind was playing midday tricks on me. He looked like the spitting image of Dorian Gray, the fallen hero in Oscar Wilde's novel who traded his soul for eternal youth and beauty. To the girls—and even guys—in my senior literature class, he was the hottest fictional character to ever get away with murder. He made evil so sexy that he made Prince Hamlet look like a wimp in tights.

I tried not to stare at Dorian Gray's look-alike. It was hard not to. His steel-gray eyes—slanted and piercing—would not let my gaze wander. The resemblance was too uncanny. He had Dorian's face—oval, angelic. His mouth was small and pouty; his lips were red and full. His hair, which was parted on the right, then combed back, was blond with dark roots. Judging by his preppy taste in clothes alone, he was definitely from the upper class.

He seemed so relaxed, carefree, the type who could strike up a conversation with a complete stranger but wouldn't be disappointed if he was snubbed.

"Mind if I join you?" he asked.

"Huh?" was the best word I could come up with from my *Dictionary of Speechless Moments*.

He pointed to the empty chair across the table from mine.

I looked around the restaurant. The place was practically empty. As in Current Occupancy: 2. Him and me.

Yet he chose to sit with me.

I consented. He pulled the chair out and sat himself down.

I went back to Oscar's play and read the same line over and over—"I suppose so, if you want to"—hoping the repetition would strengthen my concentration. It didn't.

The second I took my eyes off the book, I caught him staring at me. It was as if he'd been waiting for this moment to happen. "This sandwich is terrible," he said, making a *yuck* face.

I stifled a laugh.

He tossed the rest of his sandwich on his tray. He'd barely eaten any. "Even this kale shake is awful."

"I know," I wanted to say. But his stare kept getting in the way of my words.

"I hope I'm not disturbing you," he said. "If I am, just tell me and I'll disappear."

I shook my head. "It's fine," I said, even though his attentiveness was making me nervous. Truth is I never had anyone pay me that much attention before.

"You won't believe me when I say this, but that's my favorite play you're reading." He pointed to the picture of Oscar Wilde on the cover. It's the famous portrait of him wearing knee breeches, silk stockings, low shoes, and a velvet coat.

My ears perked up. "Favorite?"

"All-time," he said.

"You read it?"

"Twice," he replied. "It's so witty."

I yupped with a smile.

"The whole bit about bunburying is pure brilliance."

With Oscar as our common ground, I started to feel more relaxed.

"I wonder how many people in the world right now are bunburying," he said.

"If only you knew," I wanted to tell him.

"Imagine if the whole world were ruled by bunburyists," he continued.

I thought about it for a moment. "Everyone would be deceiving each other, right?"

"True," he said. "But I don't think bunburying is meant to hurt anyone. It's more about having fun, right?"

I nodded. He had a point.

Silence snuck in. It lasted for a few heartbeats; then he shattered it with "This is crazy. We've been talking for I don't know how long now, and I don't even know your name. Mine's Ran."

"Ram?" I asked.

"No," he said, laughing. "Ran. As in past tense of *run*."

"Like '*Ran* out'?"

"More like '*Ran* over,' " he said, his laughter mingling with mine. "And you are?"

"Ken," I said, "with a Z."

"Ken with a Z?" he said. "That's so cool. A name with a preposition."

"No," I said, embarrassed. "It's just Ken Z."

"What's the Z stand for?"

I paused. Now I had to hunt my mental dictionary for a Z-word, because my mother had given me none. The Z didn't stand for anything. I blurted the first thing that came to mind. "Zafar."

He furrowed his brows. "Zafar?"

"Yeah," I said, trying to sound convincing.

"That's far out," he said. "Ken Zafar."

I kept quiet, prayed he wouldn't pursue the Z issue. He didn't. Thank God. Instead, he drew a paperback from the inside pocket of his jacket. It was covered in brown paper. He tore off the cover and held the book up for me to see.

I couldn't believe my eyes. On the cover was the silhouette of a prisoner standing behind the iron bars of a prison cell marked C33. The book was *De Profundis,* by none other than our literary hero.

"Holy mackerelativity!" I exclaimed.

"Right?" he said. "I mean, how often does this happen? It's so Close Encounters of the Wonderment Kind." He laughed.

I did too.

"Oscar must be in stitches right now," he said. "This is so wild."

I laughed at the pun.

"What's so punny?" he said, laughing.

But Ran was right. How often does that happen? Two strangers meet at an uppity mall. Both end up in the same organic restaurant, ordering the same value meal. Both are carrying books by the same writer.

He placed his book beside mine. *The Importance of Being Earnest* next to *De Profundis*. One's a comedy, the other a tragedy. Two words that best describe the life of Oscar Wilde. The master of wit and humor in Victorian society, before they threw him into prison.

I asked about the meaning of *De Profundis*.

"It's Latin for 'from the depths'" was Ran's reply. "Oscar wrote it while he was in prison. It's actually a long letter to Bosie." He was referring to Oscar's lover.

I remember CaZZ and Mr. Oku talking about it briefly at our last book club meeting. I forgot the details, except that it had something to do with Oscar suing Bosie's father.

"Why did Oscar go to prison?" I asked.

"For being himself," Ran replied. And left it at that.

"The entire book is a letter?" I asked, amazed that anyone could write a single letter the length of a book. Then I remembered, of course it was possible. Because anything and everything was possible when the subject was Oscar Wilde.

"What else can a writer do in prison?" Ran asked. "Prisoners weren't allowed to talk to one another during Oscar's time."

"How barbaric!" I said. In my mind, I imagined Oscar killing time in his prison cell. Inside the four walls of loneliness, I imagined him talking to himself when he wasn't screaming in silence, or praying on a blank sheet of paper that, as days turned into months, blossomed into a book.

Ran picked up the paperback, turned it to the opening page, then passed it to me.

Suffering is one very long moment.

We cannot divide it by seasons.

We can only record its moods and chronicle their return.

I closed the book and handed it back to him.

"Heavy, huh?"

"Ten-ton truck times ten," I said.

"That's only the beginning," Ran said. "It's depressing, but I want to read it. I want to read everything Oscar Wilde ever wrote. You know, Ken Z, whenever I get the chance, I go someplace quiet and just read. Read and think."

I nodded. I could relate. I do it all the time. I'm actually at my happiest when I'm by myself, in my room or at the library, reading books, writing haikus, making lists, listening to jazz music coming from my mom's bedroom at night, and dreaming of Antarctica.

"Earth calling Ken Z," Ran said.

"Sorry." I blushed.

"Thought I lost you there for a moment."

"Nah," I said. "I was just thinking."

"About?"

"Suggesting *De Profundis* for my next book club meeting."

"You in a book club?"

"Oscar Wilde book club," I said, emphasis on "Oscar" and "Wilde."

His eyes got even wider. He couldn't believe my words. It was as if I had just delivered to him the greatest news of the century. "What? Really? No way."

I yupped and gave him my biggest smile thus far.

"Except we're still nameless," I said.

"Nameless?" He paused for a moment, then laughed. "You're in an Oscar Wilde book club that dares not speak its name."

"That's a good one," I said, remembering it was one of Oscar's famous sayings (and he had gazillions!). "Can I steal it from you?"

"It's yours," he said. "So do you go to St. John's?" Ran was referring to the exclusive school nearby. His question implied several things. He mistook me for someone who lived on the east side, someone who came from a well-to-do family. Whatever it was that made him think that, it meant I had passed the bun-burying test, that I could blend in as one of the uppity folks who hung out at Mirage.

I shook my head.

"You're not from around here?" He sounded more surprised than disappointed.

"Nope," I answered.

"A tourist?"

He took my silence for a no.

"If you're not a tourist, then—"

"I'm from Central," I said, and waited for an awkward silence to follow. None. He just nodded and smiled.

It was my turn to ask the questions.

"I'm from up north," he responded.

"North?" I echoed.

He spelled it out. "North. Kristol."

I went into mute mode. I didn't want to believe it. My face went sour, as if I'd bitten into a lemon.

Ran is from the other side of the Pula Range, a series of mountains that sprouted from the earth like green knuckles. Splitting the island almost perfectly in half, they serve as geographical

19

borders between the two Kristols—North and South. The countries, however, are not enemies. If anything, they're allies, in the sense that the south depends on the north for assistance—economic and military—as North Kristol is one of the richest island nations and has one of the strongest armies in the Pacific.

"What's the matter, Ken Z?" Ran looked dejected. My silence and sudden withdrawal had stung him.

"Oh, nothing," I said.

He didn't buy it, so I told him, "It's just that I've never met anyone from the north before."

"Is that a good or a bad thing?"

"Good," I said, which sounded more like "I guess." And although he managed to smile, I could read hurt on his face. I felt bad. Ran didn't deserve my cold reaction just because he was from Planet Privilege. He was funny, sincere, and as much a fan of Oscar Wilde as I was.

"Can we be friends?" he asked.

"Of course," I said right away. It was my one chance to redeem myself. "So what brings you to Mirage?"

"My mom works on the base," he replied.

Just then, his hair, which had managed to stay in place the whole while, fell over his face. "One of these days"—he paused to rake back his bangs with his fingers—"I'm going to cut this all off."

"No, don't," I said.

Surprised, he asked why not.

"Um . . . looks . . . Gray," I said.

My words obviously did not register because he looked at me as if I'd just spoken to him in English as an Alien's Language. He burst into laughter.

"Mind translating that for me?" he asked.

"You remind me of Dorian Gray," I said really fast. "Sort of."

"Really?" he said, blushing. "Thanks. But Dorian's got blue eyes; mine are gray, weird gray because sometimes they're light brown. Regardless, I'll take the compliment, Ken Zafar. I just hope I'll still look seventeen when I turn seventy."

"Careful, Ran," I said. "That's how Dorian got into trouble in the first place, remember? Making a wish never to grow old."

"True." He laughed. "Then again, we don't even know if the world will still be around."

"Not if Antarctica continues to melt," I said.

"And not with all these wars around us," he added. "So depressing. Hurry. Change the subject before we depress ourselves further."

"So, are you on spring break?" I asked.

"Starting today," he replied. "You?"

"Same."

"Let's hang out," he said. "That is, if you want to. Be nice to talk to someone, you know. About Oscar Wilde. It'll be like having our own book club. Just the two of us. We can watch movies, go to a café—anything."

"Um," I said, which he interpreted as an affirmative.

"Great," he said. "Do you drive?"

I threw him an are-you-serious? look.

"Well, I do," he said. "I can pick you up wherever. Cool?"

I nodded my "I guess."

"Wanna trade digits?" he asked.

"Sure," I said, then gave him my number.

"What apps do you use?"

"Talking Bubbles," I said, which I use mainly for chatting.

"You use Zap?"

"Seldom," I said. Zap texts were only good for a few hours and then they got zapped.

"How about email?"

"Email? I'm probably one of the few teenagers who still uses it," I whispered, embarrassed to be sharing such a secret. But it's the truth. Nowadays, it's all about social media, with apps like Zap, Talking Bubbles, Howzit, and Chatterboxers.

"That makes two of us," he said.

"I like writing letters," I said.

"I like reading them." He pointed to Oscar's *De Profundis* as proof.

He looked at his watch. "Hey, I have to get going," he said. He took a pen from his shirt pocket and scribbled his number on the cover page.

"Here," he said, handing me the book.

I told him I couldn't.

He insisted.

Again, I told him I couldn't.

But he wouldn't accept my no. "It's my gift to you, Ken Z," he said, putting an end to my resistance. Then he rose from the table and, before walking away, lightly squeezed my shoulder. "Send me a Zap, okay?"

I nodded.

He smiled, then walked out.

I lingered just long enough to finish reading the first act of Oscar's play. I didn't need the second, third, or fourth act anymore. I knew what was going to happen, how it was going to end—happily ever after, with the two bunburying friends discovering the biggest surprise of their lives.

I sent Ran a Zap. "As promised."

Seconds later: "Thanks, Ken Zafar! See you tomorrow?"

"Yes, sir," I Zapped back.

😊 —Ran.

😊 —Me.

MY BOOK

Many of my adventures
I borrowed from books.

Bunburying changed that.
Now I have my own thrill to tell.

A book written by Ken Z,
CEO Carpe Diem Inc.

The Difference Between North and South

Ran is from the north, which means he can come to the south whenever he pleases and not get harassed by the border patrol. It's not the same for us in the south. We can't just jump into a car and zip right through the tunnel. That's too quick and simple. Too convenient. If I want to visit Ran, I'll have to apply for a tourist visa at the North Kristol Embassy, where I'll be asked questions like: how much money is in my savings, what are my reasons for going there, where am I staying and for how long, who do I know there and where do they live?

My best friend Estelle said it once took her and her family over three hours to get their visas. They were drilled with the same questions, as if they were criminals whose only crime was going on a family vacation. And they weren't even going to North Kristol; they were headed to Hawaii. But because we don't have an airport, they had to fly out of North Kristol's. And it isn't cheap. The airport tax Estelle and her family paid cost almost half the price of their tickets. That's what happens when your own small island nation has to depend on its rich neighbor to get you off the island.

We had an airport once upon a time. It shut down a few years ago; the government simply couldn't afford to continue operating it. One by one, airline companies stopped flying to South Kristol because the government kept increasing the rent, which went straight into the pockets of the officials. After the airport shut down, the shipping port followed. Since then, everything we order from the outside world—groceries, electronics, vehicles, medicine, appliances, books, toilet paper—must first go through North Kristol's customs.

The north has access to the south, which is dependent on the north. For everything. That's the main difference between a superpower island nation and an underdeveloped one that keeps getting poorer and poorer as its government gets richer and more corrupt.

And unless the God of Role Reversal intervenes, North Kristol shall remain our only gateway to the world and our only means of returning home.

THE IMPORTANCE OF BEING A B

To be or not to
Be a bunburyist is
The bigger question.

WHAT I GET FOR LYING

Zafar: an anti-ship cruise missile

—Q<small>UICKIEPEDIA</small>™

Lightness

Waiting for Ran is more nerve-racking than waiting for the number eight bus. We were supposed to meet at seven-thirty. That was over an hour ago. So why am I still here? It wasn't my idea to hang out.

He Zapped me, so I Zapped him back and told him to meet me at Serendipi-Tea.

Maybe he's changed his mind and just doesn't have the guts to say so.

I hope he didn't get into an accident. But what if? What if at half past six, he got into a head-on collision with an army truck because he was speeding to get to me on time? What if they're still trying to pry him out of his car, which is smashed like an accordion?

I should just surrender to the Lord of No-Shows and drag myself home. What am I waiting for?

To stay or not to stay.

Finally, I make up my mind to leave.

Outside, I bump into a large man. "Oh dear," he utters, then apologizes for nearly knocking me down, even though I'm the one who went charging out of the café like a bull let loose on the streets of Pamplona.

It's Oscar Wilde. He's tall and stout, like the selfish giant in his fairy tale. His features are striking. He has a long face. His wavy hair covers his broad forehead. His large blue eyes are deep-set with thick arched brows; his mouth is full. He isn't handsome but doesn't care. He is someone who knows that physique and looks can be compensated for. That what is important is not how you look, but how well you know yourself, the suit of confidence you wear wherever you go, whomever you're with.

Oscar once quipped that if you cannot be a work of Art, you might as well wear Art. He does both. Like in his portraits, he is wearing his signature outfit: all velvet—a black velvet cape over a green velvet suit. Pinned on the lapel is a green carnation. His hair is like that in many of his photographs—perfectly parted in the middle and flowing to the base of his neck.

"Oscar? What're you doing here?"

"I came to answer your prayer," he replies. "Or have you forgotten?"

I shake my head in disbelief.

"Why the rush?" he asks. "Where are you off to?"

"Home."

"Home?"

I nod and go straight to the point. "I've been stood up, Oscar."

"Mon Dieu, mon coeur!" he exclaims. "Who would dare desert such a charming boy?"

"I'm not surprised," I say.

"Perhaps there's a reason for the delay."

"Doubt it," I say. "More like ghosting."

I'm about to excuse myself when he blocks my way. "Don't go yet, dear heart."

"It's no use, Oscar," I say.

"Wait for a few more minutes. You've already waited this long. A few more minutes won't hurt, right?"

"Another minute, Oscar, and I might turn into fungus."

"In that case, I'll join you," he says, laughing.

I make another attempt to leave. And again, Oscar persuades me to stay.

"Oh, Ken Z," he says, "don't go. Stay."

"Stay?"

"With me," he says. He points to the night sky. "The moon's just risen. And she, I am told, will be all aglow tonight."

Just then, a car honks its horn at me as it pulls right beside the curb.

"I believe your ghosty has just arrived," Oscar says, more to himself than to me. Shaking his head, he adds, "I tell you, you young ones with your never-ending quest for adventures of the heart. Until the next rendezvous, Ken Z. Ta-ta."

And before I know it, the Saint of Answered Prayers is gone, replaced by Ran summoning me to get into his car. "I'm so sorry, Ken Z," Ran says. "Thank God you waited."

"It's okay," I say.

"It's not okay," he says. "I'd be upset if I were in your shoes."

I keep quiet, nodding as he explains his lateness. "It was traffic inferno inside the tunnel," he says. "Everyone's probably heading to Mirage for spring break. Plus, there was no signal in the tunnel."

I continue listening. What else can I do? It's not like he

31

caused the traffic. All that matters now is that he's here. And I was not stood up.

As we approach a red light, he drums his fingers on my hand. "Ken Zaroo-nee?"

"Yeah?"

"Mind if we just drive for a while?" he says. "Maybe go to a park? It's such a nice night it'd be a waste if we spend it inside a movie theater. Is that cool with you?"

Of course it is. It's cool just being chauffeured by Dorian Gray's look-alike. Never would I have imagined cruising around South Kristol in a car that, before tonight, only existed in sci-fi movies and TV shows. It looks very deceiving. From the outside, it's just a plain and small, box-shaped wagon. But inside it's roomy, with wide-bodied reclining seats upholstered in soft leather.

The car runs without a key; instead of an ignition there's a red POWER button that Ran pushes to start or stop the engine. Behind the steering wheel are brightly lit, colorful panels. One is for the GPS that shows which road we're on and notifies us of any traffic or accidents in the vicinity. My favorite part about Ran's car is the sound system that makes me feel like I'm riding inside Ran's playlist.

As Ran drives us to the next chapter of the night—I want to call it "Cruising with Dorian Gray's Double"—a list of questions begins to multiply in my head:

What is Richie Rich doing with Winnie-the-Poor?

Why can't South Kristol be a phoenix and rise from its third-world ashes?

What can I possibly have that Ran's money can't buy?

Does he want to trade places with me for a day? For forever?

He can be the after-school bookworm library monitor who lives in a two-bedroom household in a run-down four-story apartment building, and I will dye my hair blond and be Dorian Gray's look-alike from up north who drives a computerized car.

What if he turns out to be the Dorian Gray of North Kristol who never gets old because he likes to hang out in the underworld and smoke opium?

Does that mean he is a sucker for vices?

Does that make me an accomplice to his vice?

Am I a vice?

"Wow, check out the moon, Ken Z." Ran stops his car in the park's desolate parking lot. I step out to get a better look at the sky. I've never seen the moon so bright and bold as tonight. Like it has nothing to hide and everything to share.

Ran and I spend most of tonight talking. Actually, he does most of the talking.

Truth is I'm really not a talker.

I much prefer to listen, or write. That's why I get along well with Estelle and CaZZ.

They love to talk; I love to listen. Estelle says it's because I'm a writer, and writers get their inspirations from listening.

That's me: Ken Z, PhD from All-Ears University.

Ran asks me about my family. As it turns out, our commonality extends beyond our mutual interest in Oscar Wilde. We are both only children. We live with our mothers; our fathers are the missing ribs in our genealogy. Mine deserted the family portrait before I was born, but Ran knows his father; he is a general in the North Kristol Army who abandoned Ran and his mother to build another family or two elsewhere. Ran thinks he's got half siblings scattered all over the Pacific Islands.

"What about your mom?" Ran asks.

"My mom?"

Where do I start? She reads a lot and listens to jazz. She's also not much of a talker. Like they say: like mother, like Ken Z. Even when we're together, we're in silent mode. And it's not because we dislike or are indifferent to each other. We don't constantly need words to communicate, because silence, too, is a form of communication. That's what I learned from her. She always knows when something is up. And for the most part, I can read right through her silence.

She once told me the problem with a lot of people is they talk so much that they've lost the ability to listen. So much so that they end up repeating themselves over and over. "If people spent more time listening, there wouldn't be so much misunderstanding in this world," she said.

"Ken Z?" It's Ran's voice, trying to fish me out from my sea of monologues.

"Huh?"

"Your mom," he says. "What does she do?"

"She's a manager in a diner on the Pula reservation," I say. "And yours works for the North Kristol Army, right?"

"Yeah," he says. "She designs military exercises."

"What do you mean?"

"Mock combat fighting."

"Mock as in fake?"

"Except it can turn real."

"The soldiers kill each other?"

He nods.

"I can't really go into it." He pauses. "Because I shouldn't. And because my mom will go ballistic if she ever finds out."

"She won't," I say.

"I thought so," he says. "You're someone I can trust, right, Ken Z?"

"Of course," I say.

From what I've read online about North Kristol and what people who've visited there have told me, the place is immaculate. It's got everything: beautiful beaches, majestic waterfalls, hot springs, paved highways, top-notch schools, opera, theater, a powerful armed force.

Supposedly, no one is poor or uneducated, so I ask Ran if that's true.

"Pretty much," he says, "because education is free."

"Even college?" I ask.

"Even college."

"Wow," I say, trying not to sound envious. Too bad I can't say the same thing about South Kristol. Though public school is free, the dropout rate is high. Most students end up quitting before graduation to work full time so they can help support their families.

"What about the poor?" I ask.

Ran shakes his head, explains there's a job for everyone, able-bodied or not, young or old.

"What about the homeless?" I say.

He pauses to think. "None," he says. "None that I've seen, anyway. We don't see them."

"What about crime?" I ask.

He answers, "Hardly."

"Really?" I say incredulously.

"Really," he says, and explains that punishment is severe, even for a misdemeanor, like shoplifting. "Or chewing gum in public."

"So that's true—about chewing gum in public?"

"Yes," he says. "They fine you. It's worse if you get caught smoking or drinking alcohol on the streets."

I wait for an explanation.

"They send you to jail," he says. "And if you break the law again, they take you straight to rehab, which is on the base."

"On the base?" I ask.

"That's where it is," he says. "And the prison."

"So they shoot you if you try to escape?" I say sarcastically.

"That's part of it," he says.

I look at him. No grin on his face to tell me he's joking.

"Is that on the Internet?" I say. "I don't remember reading that on the Web."

"Don't believe everything you read online, Ken Z," he says.

"So what's the other part?" I ask.

"Well, once you become a prisoner, you become theirs for life," he says.

"Who are *they*?"

"The military," he answers. Then he goes on to say that prisoners are trained for combat fighting, then sent off to war.

"So war is their sentence," I say.

"More or less," he says.

Then, all of a sudden, I remember reading on a news website a few months ago about a bunch of people from South Kristol who got arrested in North Kristol for living there illegally. They'd gone there on tourist visas and ended up staying and working, some for several years. I guess someone snitched on them. I forgot exactly how many of them there were, but they all lived together under one roof. I wonder if they ended up in prison and are now dead on some battlefield.

"Utopia is not so perfect after all," I say, more to myself than to him.

"It never is," he says.

The two of us sit there on the park bench, soaking up the moonlit silence.

"Ran, I have a confession to make," I say, trying to steady my words.

"Confession?"

"It's about Zafar," I say.

He gives me a puzzled look.

"The Z in my name," I remind him.

"Oh, that Zafar. Your middle name."

"Well, it's not really Zafar."

"Oh," he says.

"It stands for nothing. Just Z without a period."

"As in Ken Zero?" he says, and flashes a smile with a wink. Or what Estelle calls a "swink."

"That's me," I say. "And that's the honest-to-goodness truth," I add, hoping the bitter aftertaste of a lie will leave my tongue. It doesn't.

"Don't worry about it, Ken Z," he says. "It's nothing."

"I kind of wished it stood for something, though."

"Then make it up."

"That's what my mother said."

"And you already did," he says. "Zafar. Cool name."

"Not if it means a deadly weapon," I say. "I looked it up on Quickiepedia."

He bursts out laughing. "Good one, Ken Z."

"That's what lying does," I say.

"Well, Oscar Wilde changed his name," he says. "After he got out of prison and went to live in exile, in Paris. He became Sebastian Melmoth."

Wow, I think. *Ran knows a lot about Oscar.*

"Even his wife and two sons—they, too, had to change their names. Soon after they fled England, while Oscar was still on trial."

"Poor Oscar," I say.

"Poor Sebastian," Ran says.

"So tragic."

"Fame, fortune, fall. And all because of . . ." He pauses. "I don't want to be your spoiler. Just read it. It's all in *De Profundis.*"

"Wow," he says then, pointing to the moon. "She's getting closer and closer."

"I've never seen her this close before," I say. I gaze at her for as long as I can. It isn't like staring at the sun. No matter how bright she is, she won't—can't—blind me.

I wonder how many people in the world are watching her this very moment. I wonder how many she is guiding to their destination. I wonder how many are going crazy because of her, or howling or laughing like they're on the verge of discovering something great. I wonder how many boys and girls she's enchanting with her luminosity. Like Ran and me, sitting side by side, wondering how many wonderments there are left for us.

"Isn't she so beautiful, Ken Z?" he asks.

"She is," I say.

He casually throws his arm around me. It takes me by surprise and, for a split second, I shrink back because no one's done that to me before. But the shock quickly dissolves.

"Thanks, Ken Z," he says.

"For what?"

"For being here."

"Welcome," I say, spellbound by the moon.

It's almost midnight by the time he drops me off in front of my building. The moon is brighter and closer than ever. As if she's urging me to snatch her brightness. Take it, Ken Z. Take this ball of light, she seems to be telling me. Take it because it's already yours. If you want it.

The Zissue

Growing up, I used to wonder if the Z in my name stood for the initial of my father's first or last name. Was it Zeus or Zorba? Was it Zelig, the human chameleon? Or Zulu, the fiery and powerful soldier? Or was it Zukeran, the sweet potato farmer from Okinawa?

My mother never brought up the taboo topic. She's not the type to dredge up the unwanted past, which means I shouldn't either.

Then, one evening, hungry with curiosity—I think I was nine or ten years old at the time—I asked her in a roundabout way over dinner, "Mom, what happened to the period after the Z? Where did it go?"

"Nowhere," she replied.

"Nowhere?"

Knowing she was not going to give me the answer I was looking for, I went straight for the bull's-eye. I asked her for *his* name. She answered with a silence that equaled a thousand and one stings. A reminder not to tread on a dead zone over a fried chicken dinner. As far as she was concerned, he, whoever he was, was better off zilch, and I should get used to such emptiness in my life.

I bit my lip to hold back the tears.

She must've noticed, because she said, "Oh, Ken Z, make it up."

"Make what up?"

"The Z," she said. "You can do it. Make a Z-name for every single day of your life."

"A Z-list?"

"Exactly," she said.

"I can do that?" I asked. "Give myself names?"

"Of course," she said. "After all, it is *your* name. You have to answer to it."

End of mystery.

NAME ME Z

Ken Zeus, Zuperstar
Zeke, Zoom, Zabadabadoo
The power of Z

Case Closed

What I didn't tell Ran was that, like his mother, mine also worked for North Kristol's military at one time. This was a long time ago, before I was even born. Soon as she graduated from high school, she left Japan and went to North Kristol as a tourist. And she loved it—the island, its people, but more so her independence and the unbridled freedom that she hadn't known she was entitled to.

"Ken Z, there is nothing more terrifying than discovering you're a stranger outside of your small world," she said. "Terrifying but also exhilarating."

She decided to stick around North Kristol for as long as she could, looking for ways to extend her vacation, perhaps turn it into something more permanent. "Japan was home, Ken Z," she said. "It protected me, yet it wasn't enough."

She told me this mind-blowing part of her past on one of those few precious nights when she'd knock on my open door and talk to me freely, openly, no word limit. I'd never forgotten it, just as I try to remember every conversation I have with her. They're so rare and unexpected that it makes remembering them more urgent, necessary.

Since then she'd never gone back to Japan.

"What about Grandpa and Grandma?" I asked. "Did you ever see them again?"

She shook her head.

"I gave up the past," she said.

I asked her why, and she said that she had to. "No matter how much I wanted to turn back," she said, "I just couldn't."

"Because you had me?" I asked.

She was about to say something, then stopped herself. Her silence should've sufficed as an answer. Yet it didn't.

"Do they know about me?" I asked.

She remained quiet. I asked her again. I wanted to hear it come out of her own mouth. For her to spell it out, because to me, silence, no matter how powerful, is sometimes not enough.

Like a cop determined to nab the villain, I pursued the issue. And the more I nagged, the further she retreated.

End of conversation.

Tonight, the memory of that conversation returns to me. It plays in my head over and over and will not stop. This part of her past that's gotten me all worked up and won't let me sleep unless I bring it out into the open.

Soon as I hear the front door closing, I call out to her.

"Still up, Ken Z?" she asks, peeking into my room.

I go straight to the point. "Ma, why did you move to South Kristol?"

The question takes her by surprise. She covers it up immediately with a matter-of-fact "I was pregnant with you."

"Why didn't you stay up north?"

She takes a moment to think through her answer. She's about to say it when, suddenly, she stops herself.

"I don't see why we had to move," I say to fill her silence. "Isn't life there much easier, better?"

She looks me straight in the eye. She's annoyed, or I've upset her. She wasn't expecting me to hurl an open can of memories at her at two in the morning.

"I left North Kristol, Ken Z, because I didn't want to raise you there just so you can be stuffed into a body bag," she finally says. "If we had stayed there, the draft would've taken you away from me."

"I would've returned," I say.

She shakes her head. "They lure you with money, with dreamlike packages. But the moment you're no longer useful to them . . ." She pauses for a moment. "Trust me, Ken Z, I worked for them for five years."

"But—"

"Go to sleep, Ken Z," she says, closing my door.

"Ma?"

"What?" she says, trying not to sound exasperated.

"Can you honestly see me with a gun?" I ask her. "I mean, really, Ma?"

She takes one good look at me, then ends her inspection with a smile of relief.

Case closed.

@ Wired

"Finally!" CaZZ blurts the moment she sees me enter the diner. She and Estelle are in our usual booth at the very back, near the restrooms. @ Wired is our favorite hangout. It's one of those old-fashioned restaurants that were once the craze in the '50s and '60s. Formica countertops with stainless steel stools, booths with upholstered red-and-black vinyl seats, and, in one corner, a coin-operated jukebox that cranks out oldies but goodies.

"You got us all worried," CaZZ says. "You've never been late before."

"Yeah, what's going on, Ken Z-licious?" Estelle says.

"I overslept," I say.

"What? Ken Z? Overslept? I don't believe it," CaZZ says, eyeing me suspiciously.

"Something's different about you?" Estelle says. "I can't put my butterfinger on it. But you look . . . um . . ."

"I saw it, too," CaZZ jumps in. "Soon as he came in. He has a bounce to his walk, like the universe only weighs an ounce."

46

Pause. "Ken Z?" She pauses again, waits for me to respond. I don't. "What happened this weekend?" she finally says.

"Nothing," I say, then, more convincingly: "I swear."

CaZZ isn't buying it.

Neither is Estelle. She usually comes to my defense whenever I'm being drilled by CaZZ, but this time, she's on her side.

Finally, I let the cat out of the bag. "Okay, if you must know . . . I went to Mirage," I say.

CaZZ gasps in shock.

"You did what?" Estelle says.

"What the heck, Ken Z?" CaZZ says. "Why?"

"We already told you that place is hatrocious," Estelle says, spewing a word from *Estelle's Dictionary of Made-Up Words*.

"Those racist pigs turned us away, remember?" CaZZ says.

"Because of their stupid dress code," Estelle adds.

"I know," I say.

"I thought you didn't care about the place," Estelle says.

"You better have a good reason," CaZZ interrupts.

"If I tell you, you won't believe it," I say.

"Try us," CaZZ says.

"I went there to . . . bunbury," I say.

"OMG, Ken Z," CaZZ says, overlapping with Estelle's "Seriousness?"

I nod.

"Which means you had to dress up," CaZZ says.

My yes prompts Estelle to ask if I took a selfie.

"Get real, girl," CaZZ says. "Ken Z can't even be bothered to look at himself in the mirror."

"I wish I had been there," Estelle says.

I shake my head.

47

"It wouldn't be bunburying then," I reason.

"Yeah, Estelle," CaZZ says. "The whole point of bunburying is to get away from everyone you know."

"True," Estelle says.

"So what did you bunbury as?"

"An anthropologist"—I smile—"on a tight budget."

"Hilariousness," Estelle says.

"So how did it go?" CaZZ asks. "They treated you like shit?"

"Yeah, prithee, tell us what they thinkest of thou," Estelle says.

"Surprisingly, they were nice."

"Nice-nice or fake nice?" CaZZ says.

"I don't know." I shrug.

"They probably thought you had money."

"I did. But lunch ate up all the money I had in my wallet," I say. "So I went home. The End."

"How anticlimactic—" Estelle says.

"Then . . ." I interrupt her, pausing just long enough to irk the heck out of them.

"Then what?" CaZZ says, ready to yank the rest of the words out of me.

"Ken Z, you're killing us softly," Estelle says.

"Then I waited three hours for the bus," I lie. Actually, the bus miraculously arrived shortly after I got to the bus stop.

"That's the punch line?" CaZZ says, disappointed.

"Good cliff-hanger, Ken Z," Estelle says, laughing.

"Still," CaZZ says, "that doesn't explain why you have that dreamy look on your face."

This is the downside to having best friends. They know me so well they can see right through my daydreams.

Finally, Estelle comes to my defense. "But he always has that glazed look in his eyes, especially when he's got a haiku on his mind. Right, Ken Z?" She winks.

This is the upside to having two best friends. One of them is bound to side with me. Usually it's Estelle.

"Look at that face," CaZZ teases me. "Whatever world you're in, Ken Z, it can't get rid of that smile."

"What smile?" I say, and make a face.

"You're such a goofball," CaZZ says.

"Stop it, Ken Z," Estelle says, "you look de-mental."

"You can't wipe it away," CaZZ says. "Because it's in your eyes, too."

"Smeyes," Estelle says, "and smose and smorehead and smears and swinks."

"Whatever," I say, and roll my eyes.

"It's your aura, Ken Z," CaZZ says.

I shrug. "What aura?"

"Who cares," Estelle finally says. "Whatever zone you're in, Ken Z, don't leave it. It makes you really cute."

• • •

I still remember my first day of friendship with Estelle. Second grade. She had just moved to South Kristol from Saipan, the island closest to us. It and North Kristol are the alternative destinations for tourists who can't afford to splurge in Hawaii or Guam.

A group of boys were picking on me, taunting me with every synonym they could come up with for *nerd*. I paid no attention to them. I never understood the point in fighting back, especially when I was outnumbered. Besides, the rest of the world was already engaged in bloody, useless wars. It wouldn't be so bad if it were a word war. But it would've still ended in punches and kicks, as their vocabulary was limited to hate.

So I did what my mother always tells me whenever I want to punch the world in the face. I made a list and prayed that the hateful names left my body as soon as I wrote them down. Some did, others didn't. Because I was—and still am—some of these names. I am a *nerd*, I am a *bookworm*, I am a *geek*.

On that memorable day, Estelle told them to back off. Some did, two didn't. Mike Perez and Jimmy Burns. Bullies then, cyberbullies now. They began taunting her. As any young girl would do when pushed to the edge, Estelle fought back. Mike threw the first punch and almost hit her in the face. She went with an uppercut and got him in the gut. Mike turned beet red. He doubled over. I thought he was going to die. We all did. Tears streamed down his face. While he gasped for air, the other bully, Jimmy, tried to kick Estelle from the side, but she caught his leg just in time, pulling it so hard he thudded on his butt. Everyone laughed. Estelle could've done more damage, but our teacher, hearing the clamor, rushed into the classroom. "Shame on you," she scolded the boys, "picking on a girl." The news smacked them hard in the face.

Later that day, Estelle said, "Stick with me, Ken Z. We can protect each other." Protect each other? I could never be her bodyguard. That's what I thought at the time. But after nine years, I came to understand that being a friend doesn't mean protecting someone from just physical pain but from emotional battles, too. Even if it simply means being there to listen and hand her a box of tissues when she had an unrequited crush on a girl. That is, when she wasn't falling for a boy.

. . .

Conjure up the past and it'll slap you right in the face.

That's the minus of memory.

It doesn't only recall beauty; it also summons assholes—Mike Perez and Jimmy Burns. They strut into @ Wired and head for the restrooms. But not before they stop at our table.

"Look, Jimmy, the faggots are here," Mike says.

"Freak I am, faggot I'm not," CaZZ says. "Get it right, dumb and dumberest."

"What did you say?" Mike asks.

"I said I'm a freak of nature for modern science to correct," CaZZ says.

Mike and Jimmy look at each other as if she's lost her mind. If there is one thing that messes with bullies, it's when their targets embrace the names meant to break them. I learned that from CaZZ. "They don't have power over names, Ken Z," she once told me. They lose it once the people they're terrorizing take those names and make them theirs. Names like "queer," "queen," "freak," "dyke," "lesbo," "trans."

Estelle laughs. "Dumb and dumberest. Good one, CaZZ."

"Shut it, lesbo." Now it's Jimmy's turn to harass.

"You two want a rematch?" Estelle asks. "Come on. Let's go. One-on-one."

"Nah, I'm not into hitting tomboys," Jimmy says.

"Just say when, asshole," Estelle says.

"Whoa, dude, she just called you an asshole." Mike laughs.

51

"What?"

"Ass. Hole," Estelle enunciates. "Rhymes with black. Hole."

Estelle's and CaZZ's fighting spirits must've possessed me, because I tell Jimmy and Mike to scram.

"Whoa, Minnie Mouse has a voice after all," Mike says. "Stand up and say that."

I get up from my seat, surprising everyone, including myself. If there is one heroic moment in which I am going to stand up for my friends and look my assassins in the eye, it's right here and now. Gutsy-glory thing to do, especially since I've never been in a fistfight before. My training as a boxer takes me as far as the front-row seat during screenings of all the Rocky movies.

Mike looks me in the eye.

CaZZ stands up, but it's Estelle who steps between Mike and me.

"Come on," Estelle says, clenching one hand into a fist.

"Next time," Mike says. Then he and Jimmy turn and leave.

We all sit back down.

"Wow, Ken Z!" CaZZ says.

"Yeah, Ken Z," Estelle seconds, "wow!"

"Wow what?" I ask.

"What just happened," CaZZ says. "Where did that come from?"

I shrug. "I don't know," I say, though it feels like the right thing to have done.

"First the bounce, then the smeyes, and now you almost got a black eye from Mike." CaZZ laughs. "Pretty soon you're going to be a kickboxer, like Estelle."

"I like this"—Estelle pauses as she searches for the perfect Estellar words—"brazening side of you, Ken Z."

"Yeah, right," I say.

"You know, I used to feel sorry for assholes like Mike and Jimmy," CaZZ says, "because for all we know they're getting bullied at home."

I look at CaZZ. The scars on her face are still visible. Someone sliced it with a broken beer bottle. To this day, no one knows who was behind the hate crime.

She was already fierce when Estelle and I met her in seventh grade, but the constant bullying and beatings only made her tougher. She transferred to our school when the school on the Pula reservation shut down.

Now she doesn't care anymore. She figures if she's going to get beaten again, she might as well die fighting. "I can't let them win," she told Estelle and me when we visited her in the hospital last year. "I'd rather die than stop being me."

CaZZ, my fierce friend. The girl warrior from the Pula race.

"You know Oscar Wilde was bullied too, right?" she says. "By Bosie's father. But Oscar Wilde fought back. Even when he knew he was going to lose. He fought back. To the very end."

"That's why we love him," Estelle says. "He knew how to fight a losing battle."

CaZZ's phone beeps. "Estelle, Gramps will pick us up in front of the grocery store in an hour," she says. "You sure you don't want to join us, Ken Z? It's gorgeous there, you know. Like a tropical Antarctica," she continues, trying to entice me with Antarctica.

"Can you imagine Ken Z sleeping outdoors?" Estelle says. "I can't."

"Mount Pula is gorgeous," CaZZ says of the dormant volcano where she, her grandfather and her brothers, and Estelle will be

53

camping this week. "Plus you get to witness Estelle and me go through smartphone withdrawal."

"But you two can't live without your smartphones," I say.

"They're addictive, like drugs," CaZZ says.

"And we're Wi-Fi addicts," Estelle says.

"This camping trip will be like our rehab," CaZZ says.

"It's going to be hard," Estelle says. "CaZZ and I will probably end up murdering each other on day two."

"You sure you don't want to see us suffer?" CaZZ asks.

"Tempted," I say, "but no thanks."

"What are you going to do for a week without us?" CaZZ asks.

"More like what are *we* going to do for a week without *him*?" Estelle says.

"I'm going to read Oscar's fairy tales," I say. It's what we're reading next for the book club.

"You don't ever get lonely, Ken Z?" CaZZ asks.

"Nah," I say, which is the truth. Reading a book can turn into pages of boredom, writing haikus can be equally frustrating, and making a list can get tiresome. But they never make me lonely. "Nah," I say again.

"Nothing is ever lonely if what you're doing makes you happy." Estelle smiles. "Right, Ken Z?"

"Right."

"You can always go back to Mirage and bunbury some more," CaZZ says.

"Too bad you can't bunbury up in North Kristol," Estelle says.

"How I wish," I want to say as snapshots from last night flash through my mind. Cruising to the future inside Ran's car. Ran's arm across my shoulders. The bright moon bouncing in the palm of my hand.

"You'll miss us missing you," CaZZ says.

"Aw," I say.

"Write me a haiku," Estelle says.

"Me too," CaZZ says.

"I will." I smeyes. "I will."

Twice Beautiful

Estelle. So beautiful she's twice beautiful. Like a glam-rock model out of the pages of fashion magazines. The boys go wild over her smooth and slender neck, her chiseled face and sharp jawline, her red-wine lips and bony cheekbones, her soul-stalking panther's eyes. Until they realize she looks like them. Estelle, so gaga-gorgeous, the guys don't know whether to hate her or date her.

Girls, too, go giddy over her. As if they're coming face to face with the auto mechanic of their dreams. And when she slicks her hair, removes her rebel-red leather jacket to show them her tattoo of a serpent coiled around a rose on her right shoulder, then flashes her smirk so cocky that it's sexy, they start going cray-cray over her. Until the asteroid of reality hits them—*he* is actually a *she* sharing a locker room with them. Estelle, their third-person-pronoun nightmare. So devilishly handsome, the girls don't know whether to date her or hate her.

CaZZandra, from Roman to Greek

CaZZ should've been born with double-Xs.
Instead she was the kid who grew up with unwanted
    names.
To her mother, who went to the liquor store one afternoon
    and never came back, she was Cassius. Not Gaius
    Cassius Longinus, the Roman senator who conspired
    with his brother-in-law Brutus to kill Julius Caesar.
    Not Cassius Clay, one of the greatest boxers, known to
    the world as Muhammad Ali. But Cassius Washington
    Jr., after a stranger CaZZ never bothered to ask her
    mother or grandparents about.
To bullies, CaZZ was more than a fairy, from old French
    faerie, which means fata, or fate in Latin.
Fate of the Freakazoid.
To churchgoers, she was ABC for Anomaly, Bizarre, and
    Comic Relief.
To jocks and cheerleaders, she was damned and doomed.
To her grandparents, who ended up raising her, she was
    the light fading at the southern end of the Kristol
    tunnel. "Choose your god," her grandfather said.

*"Make a quilt," her grandmother said. "You'll need it
     someday to comfort you."*

*Not a day went by without CaZZ getting the H-treatment.
     Harassed. Headlocked. Found unconscious and
     hemorrhaging one early Sunday morning.*

*ICU x 2 months. Intubations. Transfusions. X-rays.
     Physical/occupational/speech therapies.*

Quick, MRI the Queer.

*Each blood-drawn day as cruel and unbearable as the
     next.*

*All because Jack is Jill. And believed and fought to stay
     Jill.*

Punch for punch, kick for kick, she fought back.

No matter what she did, it was a no-win situation.

*So she changed her name. Cassius, meet CaZZandra with
     a double-Z. The girl Greek gods pine for. Apollo was
     so in love with her that he ordered the snakes in his
     temples to lick her ears clean, thereby granting her
     the gift of prophecy. When she refused to return his
     love, he cursed her so no one would believe any of her
     prophecies.*

CaZZandra. Madwoman. Disregarded prophet of disaster.

*Roman or Greek, Cassius turned CaZZ is still here, day in
     and day out. Always losing, always outnumbered, always
     fighting battles she never started. Endlessly collecting
     bruises and curses to offer to the beautiful, cruel gods.*

TRIPPING

Walking home, tripping
On a moonlit memory.
Oscar, where are you?

Monday, 4 March, 4:45 P.M.

Ken Z!!!!

                    Ran?

I'm at Serendipi-Tea

                    What?!

You free?

          Give me ten.

You Are Here

The first thing Ran spots in my room is the map tacked to the wall above my bed. It is as if it were calling him.

"What's up with you and Antarctica?" he asks, standing in front of the huge map of the frozen continent.

I pause.

This is what happens when you let a new friend into your room. The door opens and he sees another side of you.

How do you explain to someone new in your life that the edge of the world is your kind of world? That you've been dreaming of Antarctica ever since you watched the documentary on the frozen kingdom featuring a cast of emperor penguins. A world so extreme from the rest of the Earth that it feels as if it is its own planet.

A vast wilderness worth exploring.

Where eternity begins.

Eternity carved in ice.

I watch his eyes travel across the room, taking snapshots of anything that catches his curiosity, then developing them in the darkroom of his mind. My books, DVDs and CDs. My Oscar Wilde collection. The desk in the corner with its pile of letters, all from colleges and universities inviting me to spend the next four years of my life on their campuses. The glass jar of pens and sharpened pencils. The lamp that keeps me company at night. The paperweight molded in the form of an emperor penguin.

"It's heavy," he says, weighing the paperweight in his palm. Then, noticing its flipper: "Ken Z, it's broken."

"I know," I say.

Ran runs one finger across the chipped glass where the right flipper used to be.

"Careful," I say.

"Did you drop it?" he says.

I tell him no, that I bought it like that.

"Was it the last one?"

"No," I say, remembering there were at least a dozen or more on the bargain rack. "But it was this chipped one that, for some reason, I picked up first."

"Did you know it was chipped?" he asks, staring at the black button eyes, red-lined beak.

"I found out the hard way," I tell him.

"It cut you?"

"Yes," I answer, "but minor." I look at the tip of my right thumb where the shard pierced it. I had to press hard on it for a couple of seconds to stop the bleeding.

"But you still bought it?" he asks, unable to take his eyes off the broken flipper.

"I did."

"You know, in North Kristol, stores are not allowed to sell anything defective, no matter how minor it is. They have to throw away the merchandise. Everything has to be in perfect condition."

"What about pets?"

"Same," he says. "They can't be sickly or deformed."

"Scary," I say. "And sad."

"Yeah."

"So you guys don't have animal shelters?"

"Unfortunately not."

He places the paperweight back on my desk.

"I dropped it once, you know," I say, whisper-like, as if I were disclosing a secret to him. "I thought it was the end of the world. I really thought so. I was cleaning my desk and I accidentally swept it off. I froze as I watched it fall to the floor."

"But it didn't shatter," he says, picking it up again.

"Not a single crack," I say. "Except, of course, for what was already broken."

"Lucky you," he says.

"It's my rabbit's foot," I say.

"No, Ken Z," he says. "Your penguin's flipper."

Ken Z Uchida
Eighth Grade
Miss Coloma

The One Place I Want to Visit the Most

The one place I want to visit the most is Antarctica. Antarctica is
so extreme and harsh it is simply unlivable. It is the coldest, driest
continent. Rain is a stranger there. By definition, it is a desert.
And like a desert, it is constantly being hit by strong and fierce
winds. These are called the katabatic winds, which can blow up to
two hundred miles per hour. They are so powerful that they can
white out everything, including the colony of emperor penguins
that has to face the storm every year while protecting their eggs.
Inside a windstorm, the world of Antarctica becomes invisible.
These winds are what shape the glaciers and icebergs of this icy
kingdom.

Despite these drawbacks, I still want to experience
Antarctica. It seems so pure and peaceful there. It's like being
in an outdoor library. In Antarctica, there are no wars to fight
or worry about. There are no fathers and brothers returning
home in body bags or innocent people getting killed, maimed, or
scarred for life. Because the only war that exists in Antarctica is
the fight to stay alive. Hypothermia and winds that pierce you
like sharp knives are the worst enemies. And because no war has
ever been fought there, Antarctica is an extremely special place.
A place where we might not need to keep praying to save our
crazy planet.

I wonder if the place we go to when we die is a little like Antarctica. Somewhere peaceful and remote and pure and undisturbed by sad prayers. A place with miles and miles of books, enough to cover the desert. Antarctica as the Book of Eternity. How cool is that?

The Emperors of Antarctica

Tuesday, 5 March

What a surprise! No Zap the whole day; then, suddenly, there's a knock on the door, and it's him wearing the face of "Surprise!" In his hands is a large pepperoni and mushroom brick-oven pizza and a bottle of Fanta Orange. I'm speechless, my mouth opened like that of the figure in Edvard Munch's painting. He says he can't stay very long, an hour at the most, because he has to attend a party he wishes he could skip, but he doesn't want to be badgered by questions from his mom.

An hour passes and he's still here, sitting comfortably on my chair and not minding about the time. Too absorbed watching *The Emperors of Antarctica* for the first time. I was shocked when he told me he's never seen this documentary about the life of Elroy and the other emperor penguins. How could he not? It's one of the best documentaries ever made, with one unforgettable scene after another:

> *Endless procession of emperor penguins marching across*
> *a desert of ice as they make their way back to their*
> *birthplace to breed.*

A crowded and noisy colony of black-and-white-feathered crooners, singing their hearts out and hoping their songs will attract a mate.

Elroy as an egg being passed delicately from his mother to his father.

Elroy's mother and the other mothers marching across a horizon of ice; they are on their way back to the sea to feed themselves for two months.

Powerful and deadly katabatic winds buffeting the colony.

Elroy's mother escaping the jaws of a leopard seal.

Lifeless penguins and cracked eggshells the day after the storm.

Reunion of Elroy's mother and father.

Breathtaking view of glaciers.

Elroy and other baby penguins lining up for their first dive.

A seagull swooping down on a group of chicks.

An iceberg, the length and size of our island, splitting.

A frozen world collapsing into the icy waters.

But the one scene that always gets me, that never fails to make the heartbeat of my world stop, is the part when Elroy's father and the entire colony of male penguins have to brave the katabatic windstorm. While some of the males abandon or drop the eggs, Elroy's father remains resolute. He stands gallantly on the edge of the circle, defying the deadly winds against all odds.

It is this particular scene that hits me the most. Maybe because, for once, it's the father, not the mother, who's in charge of the egg, of keeping it warm and safe underneath the folds of his belly, as if he were pregnant.

Seeing it again, this time with Ran, makes me think about

our own fathers. Mine who left before I was born, and Ran's, who stuck around long enough for memories to form. I don't know which is worse, actually: not knowing who your father is or knowing him long enough to remember him with bitterness. I guess it really doesn't matter, because, in the end, both of our fathers weren't brave enough to stick around and fight the katabatic storm for us.

"Amazing" is the first word Ran utters afterward.

"Truly," I say.

"I didn't know they're off on their own at six months old," he says. "Lucky them."

"Well, that's us soon," I say. "We're graduating in two months. It's all downhill from there. We turn eighteen, then dorm parties, then antisocial support groups, then nine-to-five cockroach existence, then splat. How depressing."

He laughs at my short chronicle of our lives.

"When's your birthday?" he asks.

"Fifth of July. Yours?"

"Cool. Mine's July too, the twentieth. We can turn eighteen together."

"Sounds like a plan," I say.

"You're going away for college, right?" he asks.

I shrug. "My mom hinted I should."

"But?"

"I don't know if I want to leave South Kristol," I say. "I'm not even sure if I want to go straight to college."

"What would you do?"

"If I had the money I'd travel," I reply. "Go to Dublin."

"Go on the Oscar Wilde tour?"

"Exactly," I say. "Dublin, London, and Paris, to visit the hotel where he died."

"And Père Lachaise, the cemetery where he's buried," Ran says.

"Most definitely," I say. "What about you, Ran? What university will you be attending?"

"No choice but to stay in North Kristol," he answers.

"Lucky you," I say. "At least you guys have real universities."

"I'm not going to college," he says. "Not right away, anyway."

"How come?"

"I have to serve in the military first," he says.

"For how long?"

"Three years."

"Three years?"

"Yup," he says. "It's mandatory. Guys and girls. But I don't want to."

"Can't you get exempted?" I ask. "Tell them you have asthma or a weak heart or something?"

He laughs. "It'll be difficult convincing them, especially since I'm on the swim team and the track-and-field team."

"Then leave."

"Impossible," he says, explaining that he can't get a passport until after he's completed his mandatory military training.

"Training for what?" I ask, though I have an inkling of its purpose.

His silence confirms my suspicion: war.

"Then move here," I say with enthusiasm, as if it's the best alternative plan.

"I thought of that—defecting," he says. "Maybe live around the Mount Pula area."

His mention of the west side makes me wonder just how familiar is he with South Kristol.

"But they'll track me down," he says. "Eventually, they'll find me and drag me back there."

"Not if I hide you in my room," I say.

He smiles. The kind of smile that stops the eyes from tearing up. "My Antarctica," he says.

"Yeah, this can be your Antarctica. Easily. I'll buy a foldout futon. Nobody will have to know. Not even my mom. And if she finds out, I'm sure it'll be cool—"

"They'll know, Ken Z," he interrupts.

Hope derailed, I keep silent for a while.

"That sucks," I say.

"Royally," he confirms. "But three years will fly by real fast."

"It will," I say in my best pretend-optimistic voice.

"Still," he says, "it doesn't sound half as exciting as bunburying . . . or Elroy's life."

"True."

"Your penguin paperweight . . ." He pauses. "Does it have a name?"

I laugh, wondering why I never thought of that before. It's like having a pet rock. It has a purpose. So why not? "Any suggestions?" I ask Ran.

"I think you should name him Elroy," he says.

"Elroy!"

"Elroy, who holds everything down," he says.

"Who has the world at his feet," I say.

"Who never gets left behind," he says.

"Because he's the one doing the leaving," I say.

"But the good kind of leaving," Ran says. "He leaves so he can experience the world."

Point taken.

We get so carried away talking that we both forget about the time.

He springs out of the chair and rushes out of the room. I catch up with him at the front door, where he's tying his shoelaces. Then, before bolting out the door, he throws his arms around me and leaves me with a few words. The hug happens so fast it feels as if it almost never happened. But the words did. And I'm pretty sure I heard it right when he said "us" and not "you" in "See *us* tomorrow."

Amazing?

Yes.

Adventurous?

Yes.

Sounds like a plan.

Yes.

See.

Us.

Tomorrow.

Most definitely.

The Downside to Focus

"You don't like it?" Ran says, hurt in his sad eyes. We're standing at my front door. He shakes off the rain as he closes his umbrella. It's been pouring all day. I wasn't expecting to see him today. But crazy weather makes people do crazy things. Like driving across the border with a newly shaved head.

"I do," I say, trying to conceal my surprise.

But it was his hair that made him a dead ringer for Dorian Gray. Thank God he's still got Dorian Gray's attitude and good looks. Now the wind has nothing to ruffle on his head or for the rain to slick back. Now there's nothing to hide his steel-gray eyes from the world. Now I'll have to wait until time grows every strand back.

"Be honest," he says.

"It's different," I say. I look over his new do. He did dye his hair, because it's more brown than gold now.

He laughs. "Of course it is."

"How do you feel?"

"I don't know how to explain it, Ken Z, but I feel so much

72

freer now. Lighter. I didn't know I was carrying so much on my head." Then he takes my hand and sweeps it across his scalp. Back and forth. His hand over mine over his scalp.

"Feels nice, huh?" he says.

"Yeah," I say, trying to think of words to best describe the texture. Smooth? Fuzzy? Velvety?

"Makes you want to shave your head too, right?" he says.

I pause to think, because it's never crossed my mind until now. Can I see myself with a buzz cut? "No," I finally answer.

"No?" He sounds disappointed.

"I don't know," I say. "I've never shaved my head—"

"Never?" he cuts in.

I nod.

Then his eyes widen. "Do it, Ken Z."

I look at him like he's crazy (because crazy weather makes people come up with crazy ideas).

"I bet you'll look real good," he says, though I think he's only trying to cajole me. "No, for real, Ken Z," he adds.

"I'll look like a Buddhist monk," I say.

"Then you and I can both be Buddhist monks," he says, and laughs.

I laugh too, as I imagine Ran and myself in saffron robes with beads around our wrists, bald as newborns.

"You won't regret it, Ken Z," he says. "I promise."

Wow, I think, *he's on a mission and won't let up until I concede.*

"It's such a good feeling, Ken Z," he says. "Like when a breeze blows in from nowhere and you get this ticklish sensation. It's like a ghost playing with your mind."

I pause to relish the phrase "a ghost playing with your mind." I like it. And will dog-ear it. Deposit it in my Bank of

Memories, then withdraw it when I've saved enough to make a list. Maybe I'll call it "Heart-Stopping Things That Ran Said."

"Tempting," I say.

"Then yield to it," he says. "That's what Oscar Wilde would say if he were here right now."

"Funny," I say, wondering where Oscar is at this very minute.

"Not even if I twist your arm—gently?"

"Negative."

"Can't make tonight an act of sacrifice?"

"Maybe one of these days," I finally say, hoping he'll give up.

"Awww, Ken Z." He looks disappointed. "Just say when."

"I will," I say.

He picks up Elroy, the penguin paperweight, bounces it on his cupped palm before placing it back on the desk. He stands up, his eyes traveling to the books on the shelves above my desk. He scans the collection as if he's seeing it for the first time.

"Tell me more about your book club, Ken Z," he says.

"Well, there are five of us," I say. "CaZZ and Estelle, my friends; Matt, who's this born-again jock; and Tanya, a cheerleader. Plus Mr. Oku. He's our teacher and advisor."

Then I give Ran a brief history of our still-nameless book club, how it all began with *The Picture of Dorian Gray,* which Mr. Oku had assigned to the entire class. Dorian Gray appealed to us right away. He was constantly courting danger. It was in his blood and beauty to rebel, commit vices. He made evil look sexy. We dug him so much that Mr. Oku suggested we form a book club devoted to the works of Oscar Wilde. Because if we enjoyed Oscar's gothic novel, we'd also like his plays and short stories.

"Mr. Oku sounds like a cool teacher," Ran says.

"He is," I say. "He gets us."

"He reminds me of my tenth-grade English teacher, Miss Robertson. She was the one who turned me on to Oscar Wilde. She was smart—and tough. Real tough. The students loved her. She was a role model, especially to the girls."

"Ran, why don't you start a book club at your school and ask her to be your advisor?" I ask.

"She doesn't teach at our school anymore," he says. "I think they fired her."

"Why?"

"Not sure."

"That's too bad."

"Sucks, actually," he says. "Royally."

"But there has to be another teacher you can ask."

"Nah."

I ask him about his high school, and he tells me, "I'm sure your school's more fun."

"You want a list?" I say. Without waiting for a reply, I begin with the gym pool that's got barely any water in it, and when there is, it's supplied by the rain. Lunch is as late as two-thirty, sometimes three, and eaten under the blazing sun because the cafeteria is not big enough to accommodate the thousand-plus students. You can count the number of boys' and girls' bathrooms on one hand. Science lab instruments are as ancient as the frog preserved in a jar of formaldehyde. The library's encyclopedia set is missing several volumes. But all the computers in the computer lab and library, though they're several models old and were donated by countries like our neighbor up in the north who could afford to take pity on us, are, thank God, still functioning. As for teachers, they're hit or miss. For the most part, I'm content with mine. I have Mr. Oku to look forward to every day. Sometimes all I need is those one or two teachers to make up for the rest, who don't really care to pass down their knowledge to us and only show up for work to collect their paycheck. Main thing is that I'm learning enough to fill out a college and/or McDonald's job application form.

The conditions in the south are so absurd that I cannot help but make fun of our depressing situation. Either that or I'll get depressed. Unfortunately, for many of us, we only have these two options: college or McDonald's.

"You're exaggerating," Ran says.

"Yes," I say. Stifling my laugh, I add, "But in a few years, it'll be true. What about your school?"

Ran pauses for a moment. He is probably deciding whether to start from second best to best, or vice versa.

"We start school at six in the morning," he begins.

Not sure if I heard him correctly, I toss the word back to him. "S-i-x?"

He nods.

"What time do you wake up?"

He holds up five fingers. Then he tells me he has to be neatly dressed in his school uniform, and in his seat, by six. Otherwise, he'll get a demerit. His school apparently runs on a merit-demerit system. A certain number of demerits leads to detention, which means labor.

"We mow lawns, clean restrooms, mop classrooms, serve lunches," he says.

"So you don't have janitors?" I ask.

"We do," he says, "but they supervise."

His school should come and clean mine was the first thing to come to my mind. But the more I think about it, the more I think this merit-demerit system should be enforced at our school. That way, we always have clean toilets and classrooms.

"You guys must be so disciplined," I say.

He shrugs. "We have no choice," he says. "It's either be disciplined or get punished."

"What's your favorite subject?" I ask.

"It used to be literature," he replies, and brings his memories of Miss Robertson into the conversation. "She made reading more interesting. She loaned me books that I never knew existed. *The Catcher in the Rye, Adventures of Huckleberry Finn, Fahrenheit 451,* and plays like *The Crucible*—"

"Oscar Wilde?" I interrupt.

"Oscar Wilde," he reaffirms.

"So you never read them in class?" I ask.

His "no" piques my curiosity as to what his literature classes are like.

"Mostly we read history books and books about wars."

"Wars?"

He nods. "We have to read up on all the wars in the world. Trojan, Napoleonic, U.S. Civil, World Wars One and Two, Cold War."

"You don't read fiction or poetry or plays?" I ask. "Shakespeare?"

"I read *Hamlet* and *Julius Caesar,*" he says.

For a moment, I feel relieved. Then he tells me that since kindergarten, he's been learning about the armed forces of North Kristol, its history, different branches, and its allies as well as its enemies. That qualifications for moving on to the next grade are to pass written and oral exams on these war-related subjects and a physical fitness test, all of which are conducted four times a year.

"We have to be healthy—and fit," he says. "We cannot be fat or underweight, but proportionate to our height and age."

"Skinny me would've failed," I say, imagining myself scrubbing toilets or mowing lawns for the rest of my life because I would've been stuck in kindergarten.

"And we cannot get a grade lower than a B-plus," he says.

I shake my head, realizing he and I both live in a hopeless world of extremes and excess. His school is rich and orderly, yet comes with a price: discipline is achieved mostly through fear and punishment. Mine is a hopeless eyesore of an institution, yet the students are not treated like soldiers in a boot camp and are, for the most part, free. He is assigned to read up excessively on the realities of a world that is made of war, while I am given the imaginative, and sometimes realistic, world of fiction.

Either-or.

All or nothing.

"Let's change the subject," Ran says, breaking into my thoughts.

"Yeah," I say, "let's."

"What're you guys reading next for the book club?" he asks.

"Oscar's fairy tales," I reply.

"Awesome," he says. "But I have to warn you, they're a bit of a downer."

"That's an understatement," I say. At our last meeting, Mr. Oku handed each of us a copy of Oscar's fairy tales. In one long night, I devoured each story.

"But he tells them so beautifully," he says.

"In a painful kind of way," I say.

"Oscar won't let you have it any other way," he says. "It's not an Oscar Wilde fairy tale if beauty doesn't come with pain."

Pain, beauty. "And sacrifice," I add, wondering if Ran shaved all his hair off as a sacrifice.

"Which is your favorite?" he asks.

I pause to recall the tales that are so gloomy I would never recommend them to depression-prone bookworms. Either the characters suffer or end up sacrificing their lives for the sake of love and friendship. But if I had to pick a favorite, it's "The Nightingale and the Rose," about a nightingale who flies from one garden to the next, looking for a red rose to give to the young man so he can offer it at the ball to the girl of his dreams. To win her heart, all he has to do is present her with a red rose. However, the only roses around are white, since all the red ones perished in the last storm. Enter the nightingale, who, to make the young man's wish come true, takes the advice of the white rose and stabs her breast with its thorn, until the flower is covered with her blood.

"Ouch," Ran winces, one hand on his heart. "I love that story too," he says, "but it's a little too violent for me. I keep imagining that part where the nightingale keeps singing as she pushes her breast deeper and deeper onto the thorn." He shudders again. "I'm just curious, Ken Z, why is it your favorite?"

I open my mouth while the words are still forming in my head. "I guess . . . it's because . . . Yeah . . . the nightingale . . . um . . . yeah . . . I mean it's because . . . yup . . . what the nightingale did . . . um . . . that's right . . . out of love. Not out of selfishness . . . but . . . the possibility, yes . . . to love happening . . . I mean, between the student and the girl . . . because the nightingale wanted it . . . wanted love to happen so much."

"Wow," Ran says, his eyes still squinting from trying to follow my bumpy train of thought. "I better read that story again."

Then he winks.

It's my turn to ask.

"Hmmm . . . that's a hard one . . . but if I have to choose, it would be a toss-up between 'The Happy Prince' and 'The Selfish Giant.' "

"And the winner is?"

" 'The Selfish Giant,' " he replies. "The Selfish Giant" is about a giant who, at the opening of the tale, despises children, forbidding them to play in his magnificent garden. As punishment, the god of karma turns his garden into an ice desert. "It's by far Oscar's least depressing tale," Ran says.

"I know," I say. "It even ends hopeful. The giant dies but is redeemed."

"Well, they all die," he says matter-of-factly. "All the good and beautiful ones."

"But the selfish giant didn't die painfully, not like the nightingale and the others," I argue.

"I just like it because the selfish giant undergoes a transformation."

"He has no choice," I interject. "He has to be nice to the children. Otherwise, his garden will remain frozen."

"And it's a happy ending," Ran adds.

I nod. "But still sad."

• • •

With words, time passes quickly and only comes to a sudden stop when I realize that my hand is in his. I try to free it from his grasp. He lets go but not before I feel a slight squeeze.

Urgh.

I've done it again, gotten so carried away in the world of thought bubbles that I completely forgot about the other world, the one that revolves around holding hands.

That's the downside of focus.

It doesn't know how to multitask.

I exhale a nervous laugh.

"I'm sorry, Ken Z. I didn't mean to make you uncomfortable," he says.

". . . " (Huh? I mean . . . it's just that . . .)

He gestures for my hand.

"Trust me," he says.

And I do. I watch his fingers curve into an O. He plants them in the center of my palm. I try to steady my jittering hand. I imagine that, at any time, it can fold over his, the way a Venus flytrap shuts its jaws after an insect has flown into its trap.

Slowly, his fingers fan out across my palm, his nails tickling my palm, stopping only when his hand is over mine, digit to digit. They stay there, unmoving, until his fingers glide between mine. I can feel my palm moistening. I'm embarrassed, but what can I do? His hand is already folding over mine, waiting for me to do the same.

"Not many understand, you know," he says.

I remain quiet as his thumb presses down on my palm.

I close my eyes and listen to the rain falling heavily again.

So this is how it feels, I say to myself. To have your hand held by another guy, your shaky fingers interlacing with his, your eyes closing as he presses down on the pads of your palm. You think of the hard rain returning to wash your side of the world and the people playing and stranded in it, and the faint glow of the streetlamps. You think of his hand folding and unfolding across your opened palm, his fingers grazing yours, while your heart, like a bullet train, races to the moon.

Spring Tease

Thursday morning, 7 March

Spring break is too short. Only a week. What kind of a break is that? Why can't schools take one of the summer months, like August, for example, and donate it to spring break? Nothing happens during the month of August anyway. All we do is hole up at home with the air conditioner running 24-7, or spend an entire day in a café or at the movie theater because it's too humid to appreciate the blue sky. That way, spring break can really feel like a break instead of lunch recess. That way, I don't have to panic about time running out on me.

I used to look forward to returning to school after a break. Not anymore. Now, I'm wishing for a typhoon or a hurricane to strike the island and cause major havoc so spring break can be extended for another week or, better yet, a month. I'm even hoping for a pyromaniac to set my school on fire, preferably the science labs, locker rooms, and restrooms so they can finally have their long-overdue makeover.

What am I saying? No! That's evil. I should be grateful for spring break because without it I would've never gotten the chance to go bunburying at Mirage. In fact, I should be grateful for whatever break comes my way, whether spring or lunch recess, because it's these short breaks that lead to major moments, like my meeting Ran at Mirage, and the moon that almost fell from the sky and into my hands, and Ran naming my penguin paperweight Elroy, and Ran's gentle squeeze of my shoulder, and all the other magical moments that are still new but old enough to be memories. And the best thing about spring break is that there are still a few days left before it's over.

It's De-Ken-Zee, It's De-Ran-Der-Ful

Thursday evening, 7 March

Blame my mother for the song that's been playing in my head all day. She's the mystery Claus behind the gift bag I found hanging on my doorknob this morning. She does this now and then, leaves small surprises for me to wake up or come home to. Journals, fine-point pens, movie passes, Post-its, books. This time, it's a CD—*Cocktails with Cole Porter.*

I never went past the first track. "It's De-Lovely" stuck with me de-instantly. Heart it so much, it's become the soundtrack of de-day: upbeat, playful, smart, and with a catchy melody. The best part of it all is that it's a list song about everything that is de-lovely. A ditty so de-witty, it's de-Wilde.

And if you're singing along and suddenly you forget the lyrics, no worries. You can make them up. Make your own de-list. Because it's exactly that kind of a song. Something Estelle would de-finitely go de-loco over. And if you end up getting in trouble with your English teacher, or worse, the grammar police nab you, you can blame Cole Porter for de-violation. He wrote the song. Blame Ella Fitzgerald, too. It was her de-crystal clear voice that got my morning off to a humming start.

I was not even aware I was doing it until Ran mentions it. "What's that you're humming?" he asks.

"Huh?"

And he answers by humming my hum.

". . . " (Oh, my God, I thought I was humming in my head!)

"It sounds nice." He smiles, sensing my embarrassment.

I tell him the song has been playing in my head since this morning. "And now, I can't shake it out," I add.

"Don't," he says. "What's it called?"

" 'It's De-Lovely,' " I say.

He shrugs.

"By Cole Porter," I add.

"Sorry," he says, "don't know him."

"He's this American composer who wrote a lot of Broadway musicals," I say.

"Sing it for me," he says.

I throw him a double-dose lethal look of "You got to be kidding?" mixed with "Over my Ken Z body."

And he answers with a pleading look that says, "It sounds like a fun song; teach it to me; please?"

"Do you want the neighbors to start a riot?" I finally say.

"Then can you at least play it for me?" he asks. "So I won't feel left out."

Seconds into the song, Ran, hovering over the CD player, looks up at me. His eyes are smiling wide.

"So control your desire to curse while I crucify the verse?" he says, echoing a line from the prelude.

"I know, right?" I remark. That's the other thing I love about the song—the rhyming is amazing.

He leans closer to the speakers. I keep quiet so he can hear the playful lyrics. A smile spreads across his face as the tempo picks up. I've never seen him this jumpy, bobbing his head, tapping his foot, swaying from side to side, surrendering himself to the music the way I did when I first it heard this morning.

He begins waddling around the room like a penguin, his feet tap-tap-tapping, his fingers snap-snap-snapping, his body shimmying, the song waking every part of his being; shaking up that part in all of us that wants to let go, let out, let loose.

And, boy, does he let himself loose, off to that place where he does not care what the world thinks of his voice, if he's singing and dancing on the beat or not. Off to that place where nothing matters except happiness and freedom and where making mistakes can be fun and liberating, too.

During the refrain, he joins Ella. But he makes up his own lyrics, shouting from the rooftops. "It's de-ken-zee, it's de-ran-duran, it's de-lovely!"

Then he tells me to jump in.

I do. Without hesitation, I sing along, invent, too, my own lyrics.

"It's de-ran-der-ful," I sing.

"It's de-ken-ta-loupe," Ran sings back.

"It's . . . de . . ." I pause, turn to him for help.

"Rinky-slink," he quickly tosses in, saving me just in the nick-tick of time.

"It's de-booga-loo!" I shout.

"It's de-doop-du-jour."

"It's de-creamerie."

"It's de-tour de France."

"It's de-tour Eiffel."

"It's de-ken-dy-cane."

"It's de-rang-my-bell."

"It's de-shoo-be-doo."

"It's de-wop-bam-boom."

"It's de-ken-ken dance."

"It's de-pro-fun-dis-da."

"It's de-lemma."

"It's de-victory."

"It's de-Wilde-in-us."

Like Ping and Pong, we toss de-words back and forth de-randomly. My *de-vine* for his *de-lite*. Back and forth, we dance and sing to de-beat of fun. His *de-luxe* for my *de-fine*. In and out of tune, we laugh and don't care.

"It's de-me."

"It's de-you."

"It's de-lovely."

It's that kind of a song. And no matter how lost we are in our world of made-up words, we somehow always find our way back to Ella in time to shout, "It's de-lovely!"

When it's over, we plop on my bed, our hearts thumping, the song still rocking our bodies.

Ran is lying on his stomach, his face buried in my pillow.

I am on my back with my eyes to the ceiling.

The two of us catching our breath.

Then he flops his arm across my chest, his hand gently pat-pat-patting my face.

I turn to my side, tap him on his buzzed head, my palm bouncing lightly against the prickly ends of his day-old hair.

He lies on his side, his eyes fixed on me while mine try to wander off. But, like a refrain to a song, they always return to his gaze. We lie there, face to face, our bodies barely touching, just lying very still and listening to our breathing that can't seem to slow down, defying silence with the sound of two thousand hummingbird heartbeats.

He smiles.

I smile.

He winks.

I blink.

He squeezes his face shut.

I wrinkle mine.

He closes his eyes. He lies there, very still, and with his shaven head, he looks like a newborn baby who wakes up to greet the world, then returns back to sleep.

Eyes still shut, he takes my hand, interlacing his fingers with mine, then buries our clasp under his cheek.

He pretends to be asleep, my hand pillowing his dream.

He doesn't let go.

I don't let him.

The two of us waiting for the calm before a de-lovely storm.

The First Certainty

MONDAY, 7 MARCH. LATE NIGHT. MY BEDROOM.

ME: I think I'm going . . . I don't know . . . Am I . . . Is this how it's supposed to . . . What . . . If I . . . Oh, forget it.

OSCAR: Heavens to Betsy, Ken Z.

ME: Who's Betsy?

OSCAR: Never mind—she's dead. But, dear heart, why am I being summoned to the palace of your imagination at such an ungodly hour?

ME: I can't sleep, Oscar.

OSCAR: Insomnia seems to track me down wherever I am.

ME: It's my mind, Oscar. It doesn't want to stop thinking—about him! It doesn't want to stop remembering.

OSCAR: Ah! Do you want it to stop?

ME: Not really. But I'm going hazy-dizzy-crazy. Am I?

OSCAR: Passion makes one think in a circle, Ken Z.

ME: Mine is a three-ring circus.

OSCAR: Marvelous.

ME: These past two nights felt like that: my mind twirling, my heart skipping, the hours speeding so fast, like I'm on a bullet train to the moon. Is this normal? Or is this the speed of madness?

OSCAR: Such is the atmosphere of Desire, dear heart. It can be neither contained nor controlled. It doesn't know how. It's not meant to be still. It has to roam, drift, follow its whimsical and restless nature.

ME: So I don't have a choice?

OSCAR: None, I'm afraid. No choice but to surrender and follow its moody and wild ways.

ME: What if it stops?

OSCAR: Think no such thoughts, dear boy. Desire cannot—and should not—be tampered with. Don't mar this wonderful haziness, Ken Z. Roll and laugh and sing with it. I know you can. You are brilliant and imaginative and de-lovely. Enjoy these blissful moments of uncertainty.

ME: Blissful? Uncertainty?

OSCAR: *Mais oui.* Uncertainty is the very essence of romance. It makes the heart of your story more interesting, exhilarating, mysterious.

ME: Terrifying.

OSCAR: As it should! Elements that are richly lacking in literature nowadays. The Messy Room of Uncertainty traded off for the Royal Palace of Scripted Anxieties.

ME: Uncertainty is the very essence of romance.

OSCAR: Yes, dear heart. It is its very essence.

ME: I'll keep that in mind, Oscar. *Merci beaucoup.*

OSCAR: My pleasure, dear boy.

Seven Steps to Eternity

Friday, 8 March

Tonight is the night of firsts.

It's the first time I slick back my hair and put on my brand-new pair of ankle-length pants to go with my checkered polo shirt.

It's the first time I wear my shirt with the top button undone.

It's the first time I smile in front of the mirror and a stranger who looks like the spitting image of me smiles back.

And if I want to, I can go back to Mirage and bunbury again—this time, with the confidence of a high-powered advertising executive.

It's the first time another guy stands beside me in front of the mirror and looks straight at my reflection.

It's the first time I feel the lightness of meaning.

It's the first time anyone has taken this much interest in me, not counting CaZZ and Estelle.

It's the first time a guy asks me if I've ever kissed someone.

I want to run out of my room.

Out of this world.

I don't.

It's the first time fear has worked in my favor.

How can I possibly answer Ran's question? What do I know about kissing, except from the Chet Baker song my mom plays late at night soon after she gets home from work? The one where Chet, in his raspy, love-tired voice, sings about lips that taste of kissing.

The answer's easy. Two-letter word, yet the most difficult one to say, and hear. Steering my eyes away from his gaze, my voice finally cracks a "no." After that, all I want to do is dive deep into one of the underwater volcanoes that surround our island.

And it's right then that I finally realize his hand is folded over mine. He's done it again. He's taken my hand while my mind went wandering off, tightening his grasp as I'm about to pull away.

"Just a little longer, Ken Z," he says. "Please."

Then he gives me one of those nervous smiles you give to the person you like and you hope will like you back.

"I only wished that it had been, you know . . ." He pauses as his voice starts to break. "That it mattered. That it began like this," he continues.

What mattered? What happened? I want him to tell me so I can understand the sadness in his eyes, and why, suddenly, he became very quiet, his grasp loosening as if he's retreating into his own world. For a moment, I think he's going to let go.

He doesn't.

Instead, he unfolds my right hand and, like a web, spreads it over his face, until all I feel are his lips, like gills, pulsing against the cup of my palm. With his hand over mine, he guides

93

them over his brows, his closed eyelids, his cheeks, his mouth breathing into my palm, his warm breath moistening my life lines.

"Ken Z," he says, taking my hand from his face and holding it between his hands. "Be random with me."

Be random? What does that mean? Be with him? Be spontaneous? Like a Ken Z list unraveling? Like being assaulted by ten thousand thought bubbles at once?

My heart begins beating rapidly. Like a panther that upon waking from a deep sleep, finds itself trapped inside a cage and starts to grow wild with fury.

Thank God Oscar Wilde shows up, all dressed up in his dandy outfit and green overcoat, the one with fur trimmings.

ME: Oscar! Oh, my God, where have you been?

OSCAR: At Père Lachaise, dear heart, attending to my daily pilgrims. Why, what's the matter?

ME: My heart.

OSCAR: Ah! Temptation!

ME: What should I do?

OSCAR: The only way to get rid of temptation is to yield to it, dear boy. Resist it and your soul will grow sick with longing.

ME: But I'm scared.

OSCAR: Fear, Ken Z, is the godchild of beauty and danger. It is Youth being summoned to the witness stand of Experience. Youth—that brief but magnificent and utterly deceiving season in our lives. It doesn't last very long, so waste it wisely.

ME: I'm afraid, Oscar. What if—?

OSCAR: My dear, nothing has to happen if you don't want it to. But you are in the midst of your own glorious unfolding.

I say surrender and enjoy the pulse of a blossom. How I envy you, Ken Z.

ME: Envy?

OSCAR: To be right in the eye of desire.

ME: It's all terrifying and confusing.

OSCAR: It's all uncertainty and wonderment. And humming-bird heartbeats.

ME: My heart is ready to jump out of my chest.

OSCAR: You must let it, Ken Z. Be open to his affections. Such devotion and attention he bestows on you. Puts Zeus and Ganymede, his cupbearer, to shame. But let's save our words for later. It's time now for you to feast with panthers.

"Be random for me, Ken Z," Ran says.

"For you?"

"For us," he says.

"Us?"

"YES. US."

"!!!???" (???!!!)

My world is suddenly reduced to a fantastic blur.

Like a cat, he nuzzles my cheek, my neck. He laughs. I laugh.

The. End.

Wrong.

Because, without a warning, he plants a wet smack on my lips.

And then another.

I want to pull away, but I'm in too much shock. Totally un-prepared. And embarrassed: my lips are chapped.

I want the night to run away, for us to start all over.

I can feel my insides turning. My legs weak and rubbery, my hands trembling. My face flushed from embarrassment.

"Ken Z, it's okay," he says, and holds my face. He looks into my eyes and smiles the kind of smile that comforts you before you're about to cry.

"Hey, Ken Z—" He wraps his arms around me. I don't know what to do with my hands, where they're supposed to go. We stay there, in a one-sided embrace for I don't know how long, until I realize we're swaying with my hands resting lightly on his back.

Then, releasing me from his arms, he tells me to close my eyes. I shut them tight. Lost as ever. This time, a little less terrified.

With spotted kisses, he anoints my forehead, my closed lids, my cheeks, and, finally, my mouth; his rapid breathing letting me know that the fear and thrill are mutual.

A kiss is a magical thing. This is the first lesson I learn about kissing. It turns fear into fantastic, danger into beauty, uncertainty into comfort.

With his tongue, he tempts my mouth to open a little and play. Suddenly, our tongues collide. Or rather his tongue sweeps over mine. I freeze. It feels weird. He does it again. And again. Like he's telling me something urgent, a secret code he wants me to learn fast. I don't know what he wants. I try to pull away, but he tightens his hold around me, his face pressed against mine. As I slide my tongue out of his mouth, he scoops it back with his mouth as if he's going to swallow it.

• • •

96

The second lesson: In French, *langue* means "tongue," "language." Tonight, language is a hunger playing with fire.

A strange feeling, kissing is. But I'm glad for the blur. Glad that it's happening with Ran, who steadies me firmly with his embrace, until he feels my arms wrapped tight around him.

Like a student eager to learn more, I replay the night's first lesson for him.

Back and forth, our tongues send each other messages, speaking to each other in our own codes for Give and Need. Hunger and Fire.

The third lesson: kiss like you're telling a story with another person, in a language that's completely yours, with the two of you making it up as you go along.

Ran changes the tempo. I quickly follow. Seconds later, it's his turn to surrender to my lead. Time ticks to our tongues taking turns flicking, rushing, exploring to feed the craving. Round and round our tongues go, coaxing and chasing each other. His hands cradling my face; my fingers caressing his back.

The fourth lesson: Kissing is like jazz. It, too, has its glorious rough spots.

Curious to see what he looks like kissing me, I open my eyes and am surprised to see a pained expression on his face. He looks like a lost child. He stops because I must've stopped, too puzzled and sad to continue. He smiles to ask me what's wrong. I smile back to say I'm not sure. Then he releases me from his grasp.

I thought the lessons for the night have come to an end,

when, suddenly, he takes my face in his hands and blows a blast of air into my mouth. I taste it. Warm, sweet, crave-able.

The fifth lesson: kissing is a mirror, watching and being watched.

Before I know it, we're tasting each other's lips again, swallowing each other's breaths again, getting lost, then found, then lost in each other's sigh again, our tongues going in circles, chasing and teasing and changing the speed of our want again. All for a beauty that once caused so much fear and unease and nervousness. And in the end, it turns out to be a magnificent blossoming. This dangerously delicious jazz called kissing.

The sixth lesson: kissing is like playing a crazy game of conquest and surrender.

Tonight, we kiss for what seems like forever, until the heart, like the panther it is, returns to its cage.

The seventh—and final—lesson: kiss as if it's the end of eternity.

Skyrocketing

Saturday evening, 9 March

I, Ken Z, am now a big question mark. Did I just kiss a boy? Yes, and it felt like a hundred million volts of electricity surging through my body.

I didn't know a kiss could be this powerful. That it could send my heart skyrocketing to the moon.

Prior to Ran, I thought the power of a kiss only existed in fairy tales about frogs and poisoned princesses.

So does this mean I'm gay now?

Am I the *B* in the LGBTQ?

But which *B*? Bisexual? Bicurious? Bromancer?

Should I kiss a girl just to be sure?

Maybe I'm the *Q* in "queer," but most definitely not "queen" since I cannot picture myself donning a tinfoil tiara.

Maybe I'm the *D* in the Multiple Choice of Sexuality, as in (D) All of the above.

Or (E) A new category.

Yes, *E*.

I, Ken Z, as my own category.

The Am I or Am I Not? Checklist

I'm fashion-unconscious.
I don't go to school looking like Miss Universe or
  Universal Show Queen.
I don't wear a gigantic flower behind one ear.
I'm actually allergic to pollen.
I don't sashay on sidewalks, crosswalks, and broken
  boulevards like a runway model.
I don't have a closet I can run to and hide.
I don't cover my arms with thick, rubbery friendship
  bracelets.
I think figure skating outfits are atrocious.
I can't disco-dance to save the '70s.
My sandal heels are less than a quarter inch.
It doesn't take me all morning to style my bedhead.
I'm a gay men's chorus's nightmare.
I'm too shy to pee in public urinals.
I prefer watching tennis over gymnastics and synchronized
  swimming.
Nude sketches, male or female, do nothing to my
  pulse.

Underwear ads don't turn me on.
Sweaty jocks give me hives.

All I know is I like Ran.
A lot.

The Secret to a Brighter Universe

SATURDAY, 9 MARCH. LATE NIGHT. MY BEDROOM.

ME: Oscar, can you keep a secret?

OSCAR: You've come to the perfect person.

ME: It's about Ran.

OSCAR: Oh dear.

ME: Yeah.

OSCAR: Go on.

ME: I think I like him, Oscar.

OSCAR: You think?

ME: Yeah, I think so.

OSCAR: You sound unsure.

ME: Do I? How can I be sure?

OSCAR: Let's start with the symptoms.

ME: Well, at night, I toss and turn because of him. During the day, I'm walking around in a daze; the world around me is hazy. I daydream more now because of him. When he crashes into my thoughts, my bad days are no longer gloomy. It's like that when I'm with him. But more intense, more magnificent.

OSCAR: I believe, my dear child, that you're afflicted with the marvelous malady called Love.

102

ME: Love?

OSCAR: When you speak of nights endlessly tossing and turning, and days swinging and dancing, and all because of one person, the very same one who governs your moods and brightens your dismal days, that, my dear boy, is due to love. It makes us feel good about ourselves. We become wiser because of it. We become better individuals because of it. We become nobler because of it.

ME: So I'm in love?

OSCAR: Is your heart a lively cage of hummingbirds?

ME: Yes.

OSCAR: Recurring daydreams and head rushes?

ME: Yes.

OSCAR: Then you are indeed, most definitely, with utmost certainty, in love.

ME: Actually, it feels good to have another person in my small universe.

OSCAR: Your world, Ken Z, is larger than you thought. It has always been. And now, with Ran, it's become even larger.

ME: Because of him?

OSCAR: Because of love, dear heart. Because of love.

SURFACING

With his hands and breath,
I draw closer and closer
To another me.

The First Days of Forever List

You forget to set the alarm clock.
You wake up late on the sunny side of the world.
Bonjour *means "Good morning, mon amour."*
You call in sick to the universe.
You forget the public library's hours of operation.
You mistake one librarian for another.
You can't come up with a name for your book club.
You rechristen yourself Ken Zoom.
You talk in your daydreams.
*You start creating what-if scenarios, but all versions end
    happily.*
"You Light Up My Life" is your new ringtone.
*You surprise the neighborhood with your hidden tenor
    talent in the shower.*
You can't—don't want to—eat.
It's okay.
You can't—don't want to—sleep.
Even better—more time for head rushes and memories.
*You track down the scent of his cologne to the nearest
    strip mall.*

You ask the salesclerk for a box of samples of it.
You reek of Eternity eau de toilette.
Inhale Ran, exhale Ken Z; inhale Ken Z, exhale Ran.
You invent a hundred body languages.
No news, good or bad, can wipe the smile off your face.
For once, you're staring at sexy in the mirror.
For once, your confidence is made of steel.
You thank the angel playing with your heart.
You wake up for only one reason.
Your world brakes for the same reason.
You answer only to one voice.
His.
Ran.
And only his.
As in Be random
With me.
Unless the gods
Are lying.
Right now.
Unless the heart.
Is pretending.
Unless.
Unless.

THE BOOK
OF FALSE STARTS

DAYDREAMS

The curve of your lips
The sigh that completes a kiss
Ah, the endless Ahs!

This

Sunday afternoon, 10 March

Ran and I are in my room. He's in his favorite chair and I'm sitting on the edge of my bed.

"I can't . . . live . . . spring . . . ache's . . . over," I say.

"Ken Zan, can you reboot?" he asks, laughing.

I look at him, puzzled.

He rolls his chair toward me. "Can you please reboot? Transmission is a little choppy. You keep breaking up." He plants a wet kiss on my lips before rolling his chair back with a kick.

"I said I can't believe spring break is over." This time, the words rush out, loud and clear, in one breath.

He looks at his watch. "It's not yet over. We still got a couple of minutes left."

"It's too darn short," I say.

"I'm going to miss driving to you every day, Ken Z."

". . . " (You can always defect!)

"This is the best spring break ever," he says, rolling his chair forward and almost crashing into me. He takes my hands and interlaces his fingers with mine. A perfect clasp. "The best ever."

"Mine too."

He releases my hands, and with his forefingers, draws circles on my palms.

"I'm going to keep seeing you until you get tired of me, Ken Z," he says.

"Or you get bored of me," I say.

He shakes his head. "Me get bored of you? Never! Nobody understands me like you do, Ken Z."

"I wish summer were here already."

"We don't have to wait for summer. We'll Zap each other. You tell me how your day went and I'll do the same. It'll be as if we spent the day together. Deal?"

"Deal."

"Ken Z—"

"Yeah?"

"Can we keep this between us?"

He doesn't need to explain further. I know exactly what he means. This room, our own private Antarctica, just the two of us, my hand in his, his head on my chest, my heart beating in his ears, his mouth on my neck, his body dreaming beside mine.

This.

Us.

Perfect clasp, perfect moon, perfect kiss. Everything perfect. Even Elroy with his broken flipper.

"Not even to your friends, okay?" he says. "I know you're very close to them. But let's not let anyone in."

"I won't."

"Promise?"

"Promise." Not a peep to Estelle and CaZZ about this new and strange happiness. This dizzying and exhilarating and amazing bliss that I have to safeguard from the outside world. So I can continue feeling this unbelievable head rush. This wild silence. This hummingbird heartbeat called Ran & I.

The One-Sided World

Ran has been driving to South Kristol for a week now. In and out of the tunnel. Up and down the island. He doesn't mind, says, "It's worth the drive, Ken Z." But I want to see where he lives too. I want to see where he hangs out, the school he attends, the park he goes to moon-gaze and read and think. I want him to sneak me into his bedroom, in broad daylight. I want to know if his bed is tucked in the corner, away from the sunlight, like mine. I want to see if his desk faces the window, or if his walls are blank or crowded with posters and paintings and maps. I want to see his library, if the books are organized by genre or author's last name. What about his collection of Oscar Wilde? Are they out in the open or hidden under the bed? I want to lie on his bed, sit in his chair, peek in his closet. I want to be part of his room. The way he's become a part of mine. I want to know what his world looked like before he entered mine. I want to make some kind of difference, leave an imprint of my face on his pillow. Something that bears a single unit of memory, something that says, "I know, because I remember."

RECURRING DILEMMA

You up north, me down
South. Between us, soldiers and
Knuckles of mountains.

Spiffy

Sunday night, 10 March

Sunday is almost over. My mom just got home. I suspect that she suspects that I'm up to something. That's me and my mom: synchronized suspicious minds.

Tonight, for example, she stops by my room to check in on me. Before walking away, she smiles lightly and tosses the word *spiffy* in the air. Spiffy? Me? I think I know what she's trying to tell me. To be sure, I look it up in *Ken Z's Dictionary of Style*. And she's right. I am *fashionable*. I am *styling*. Ken Zoot Suit.

Minutes later, I hear the soothing voice of Frank Sinatra singing "The Way You Look Tonight" coming from her bedroom. I close my eyes, and through the walls that separate our rooms, I listen as the blue-eyed crooner serenades my mother. In his story-like voice, he tells her that when he's feeling down, all he has to do is think of her, then he'll be fine again. I can relate. I do the same thing, too, when my day is ruined by bullies and bad news. I turn my thoughts to the people I care about—my mom, CaZZ, Estelle, and now Ran—and I start to feel better and lighter and grateful for the warm glow they comfort me with.

115

SENT SUNDAY 3/10, 7:31 P.M.

Home from Mt. Pula.
Lots to tell.
Zap me.

SENT SUNDAY 3/10, 8:29 P.M.

Hello? Are you there?
It's just me, your Estelle.
Nada enchilada.

SENT SUNDAY 3/10, 9:03 P.M.

Nine-o-three p.m.
Still—no Zaps, no texts, nada!
Where is my haiku?

SENT SUNDAY 3/10, 10:44 P.M.

CaZZ is sick—bad cold.
I think I'm getting sick too.
Wanna play hooky?

Uneventful

First day of class. Uneventful. High school life is really boring without CaZZ and Estelle around to bitch about it. CaZZ is down with a bad cold and Estelle decided to play hooky. I should have stayed home myself since all I did was check my phone constantly for Zaps from Ran. None. I already Zapped him four times. I wonder if he's received any of them. He must have. At least one, for sure. I sent them hours apart from each other. One last night, another this morning, the third during lunch recess, the fourth just a minute ago. But no reply. He probably passed out from exhaustion. He did not leave until way past his bedtime and he had to be in school by six this morning. Poor guy. Hope he made it to class on time and did not get a demerit because of me. But what if—? Nope, I'm not going to entertain questions I don't have the answers to.

SENT TUESDAY 3/12, 7:10 A.M.

Ken Zeeeeee!
You're killing me softly
With your silence.

SENT TUESDAY 3/12, 3:44 P.M.

How was school?
Miss me?
SOS!

SENT TUESDAY 3/12, 7:44 P.M.

What you doing?
Wanna play staring contest?

SENT TUESDAY 3/12, 10:01 P.M.

Save the whales.
Zap me.

SENT TUESDAY 3/12, 11:15 P.M.

RIP: Estelle and Ken Z.
☹
Just kidding.

Ken Zapless

Tuesday, 12 March

I did good today. I never knew I had the power to control myself. I only Zapped Ran six times over a span of twelve hours. Not bad, considering he hasn't sent me a single Zap! I hope he doesn't think I'm needy—or worse! Maybe that's why he's no longer responding. Maybe he only saw me as a spring break friend, someone to hang out with for a week, then adios, amigo. But what if he never made it back home Sunday night? What if he got into a major accident and is now fighting for his life in a trauma unit? Or worse: What if he was a bunburyist who found the perfect victim in me? But what if I'm building a tower of anxieties for nothing? What am I doing? I've got better things to worry about. Like my unfinished lists and haikus and Oscar Wilde's *De Profundis* to read and names to come up with for the book club and more beautiful memories and uncertainties to look forward to.

Gutter and Stars

Wednesday afternoon, 13 March

South Kristol High School library. CaZZ's and Estelle's first day back at school after missing classes for two days because of a head cold (CaZZ) and laziness (Estelle). The last time we were together was over a week ago, right before they were about to go camping on Mount Pula with CaZZ's grandfather and brothers.

"Imagine, Ken Z, five days without a phone?" CaZZ says, her dramatic eyes beaming at me. "It was like living in the dark ages of the '90s."

I shake my head. That's all I can do. Thoughts of Ran keep derailing me from enjoying myself with Estelle and CaZZ. I don't see them in over a week, and now that we're all in the same room, my mind is on him, worrying about him. If only he'd Zap and let me know that he's okay, then I, too, can go back to being okay.

"We gave a new meaning to the word *wireless,*" Estelle continues.

"It was just us, nature, and Pula," CaZZ says, referring to the goddess of volcanoes who gave birth to the island millions of years ago, way before outsiders came and stole it from her people. First the explorers, then the missionaries, then super-power countries purporting to be allies.

"I thought I would go cray-cray up there," Estelle says.

"But she ended up loving it," CaZZ remarks.

"Every minute of it," Estelle says. "I didn't know I was a closeted nature freak, Ken Z."

"I didn't know either," I say, trying to stay focused.

"Of course, we could've easily walked down to the reservation if we were so desperate," CaZZ says.

"But what for?" Estelle asks.

And CaZZ answers with: "So we can be reminded that we live in a violent, pro-apocalyptic, hopeless, senseless, culturally insensitive, homophobic, misogynistic, environmentally uncon-scious, fake-news-driven, doomed-from-the-very-start world?"

That's CaZZ. Once she gets started, there's no stopping her adjectives.

"Amen to that, sister," Estelle says.

They high-five each other.

It's good to see them again. They almost make me forget about Ran.

CaZZ and Estelle.

Different as sun and moon, yet they depend on each other to finish each other's sentences, complete each other's thoughts.

Like Siamese twins separated at birth.

Then reunited under third-world conditions.

And when they tell a story, they take turns supplying the details. It's like watching a tennis match, my head moving back and forth from one storyteller to the other.

"I loved being up there, Ken Z," Estelle continues. "It was so calm—"

"So serene," CaZZ jumps in.

"I almost forgot I was in the island of tropical depression," Estelle concludes.

"It's a very special place in my heart," CaZZ says.

"Very mystical," Estelle says, "like you're communing with a great force."

"Because you are," CaZZ asserts.

"I still can't believe it—a week without your smartphones," I say.

"It was hell in the beginning—the withdrawal," CaZZ says. "That's how addicted we were to these gadgets."

"Practically slaves to apps and up-and-downloads," Estelle says.

"You're lucky you don't have this problem, Ken Z," CaZZ says.

"Yeah, Ken Z," Estelle seconds.

Ha! If only they knew how, in one night, I went from anti-apps to a Zap junkie!

"Yoga helped a lot," Estelle says.

"You? Yoga? Really?" I can picture CaZZ doing warrior poses atop Mount Pula. But Estelle? No way. She's more the adrenaline-pumping kickboxing type. She'd rather karate-chop a bully than be caught dead lying on her back with her eyes closed, lifeless as a corpse. But Estelle is nodding her head and looking at me wide-eyed, like she can't believe it either.

Estelle and CaZZ then go on to describe what their day was like up in the sacred mountain. In the morning, they went for a hike, then swam in the clear pool at the bottom of Pula Falls. After lunch, which consisted of fresh fruits and vegetables that came from CaZZ's grandfather's farm, they napped or read Oscar Wilde's fairy tales in their tent. Dinner was usually grilled vegetables and barbecue chicken.

"At night, we gathered around a campfire and CaZZ's grandfather told us stories," Estelle says. These were myths and legends that, according to CaZZ, the native Pulas had preserved and passed down generation after generation through the art of remembering.

CaZZ's grandfather is one of the remaining natives who are one hundred percent pure-blooded Pula. Most of the Pulas have intermarried with other races who'd settled in the islands—missionaries from Europe, plantation owners from North America, laborers from Asia and Portugal and Latin America, immigrants from Africa and Central America. CaZZ and her brothers are mixed; you wouldn't be able to tell what they are or where they came from just by appearance alone. CaZZ is dark-skinned, but the color of her eyes is sometimes ocean green, sometimes blue, while both of her brothers have fair complexions and slanted blue eyes. Looks aside, they identify as one hundred percent native Pula.

"On our last night, CaZZ's grandfather did a chant," Estelle says. "Oh, my God, Ken Z, it was so hauntingly beautiful. Definitely the highlight of my trip."

I ask them about the chant.

"It was about the volcanic goddess Pula losing one of her children," CaZZ replies. "Her grief was so powerful that, from the bottom of the sea, she erupted for millions and millions of years. That's how this island came to be."

"Out of rage," I say.

"And grief," Estelle adds.

The chant reminds me of CaZZ and the time she lost her grandmother, less than a year ago. CaZZ was still recovering from the beating that almost killed her, when her grandmother suffered a heart attack and died. She was the rose that bloomed beneath CaZZ's wounds and sadness, the suit of armor that protected her from hurting herself whenever the bullying got unbearable. So when she died, we were afraid that CaZZ would do something crazy. But instead she grew tougher, more defiant. It was as if her grandmother had taken all of CaZZ's weaknesses to her grave and replaced them with the spirit of an ancient Pula warrior, for the Pulas were known as the warriors of the Pacific.

"Grief can do that to you, Ken Z," I remember CaZZ telling me. "It can crush you to pieces, then bring out the strength you never thought you had."

I turn to CaZZ, shrouded in silence. Usually she's the one who attracts the spotlight, doing most of the talking and leading. She says she can't help it. It's the Aries in her, the fire that comes with being a ram. Always ablaze, always taking charge.

But sometimes she gets very quiet, reflective. Like now. That's her listening and thinking and honoring her grandmother's spirit and the spirits of her ancestors and their goddess Pula. And preserving their memories through chants and stories.

"Oh, guess who we saw at the protest rally?" Estelle says.

"What rally?" I ask.

"You mean you don't know, Mister Walking Quickiepedia?" Estelle says, feigning shock.

"I'm appalled, Mister Current Events," CaZZ adds.

I shrug.

CaZZ tosses me a hint with "The observatory?"

"Dunno."

"It was all over the news," Estelle says.

Finally, they spell it out. A large crowd of native Pulas and local activists were protesting the building of an observatory on top of Mount Pula. Apparently, Mount Pula is one of the few places on Earth that offers an amazing view of the heavens.

"North Kristol wants to build it, but it's supposedly a joint venture with our corrupt government," CaZZ continues.

"North Kristol?" I ask.

"Who else?" CaZZ snaps. "They already took over the east side and renamed it Mirage. Now they want to occupy Mount Pula by planting their telescope on it."

"Pretty soon it's going to be the invasion of the North Kristol snatchers," Estelle says.

For our sake, I hope "soon" means a hundred years from now. I can't imagine living among, or being governed by, warmongers. If they take over the south, there will be no need for a border—maybe a fake one. It'll also mean being forced to join the military right after high school and not getting a passport until after the service. Without a border, Ran and I will be able to see each other more frequently, that is, if we make it back from the war whole and not maimed or messed up in the head. And what kind of life would that be?

"So who did you see at the rally?" I ask.

"Mr. Oku," Estelle answers.

"He's so cool," CaZZ says of our literature teacher.

"*Très* cool."

"And you know what?" CaZZ pauses for the surprise effect. "He came out to us!"

I keep silent, though I have a clear idea of what CaZZ is talking about.

CaZZ spells it out. "He's gay, Ken Z."

"Mr. Oku? Nah," I say.

"How would you know, Ken Z? You're a plant!" Estelle jokes.

"He actually came out and said it?" I ask.

"Of course not," CaZZ says. "Teachers don't come out to their students. They just introduce you to their *roommate*." She makes two antennae with her fingers to emphasize *roommate*.

"My gaydar is usually ninety percent effective," CaZZ says. "I knew Mr. Oku wasn't straight. I just thought he was a bachelor for life."

"Me too," Estelle says.

From Estelle and CaZZ, I find out that Mr. Oku was born and raised in Nigeria. In the capital city of Abuja. After he graduated from Oxford—he majored in Victorian literature and did his thesis on Oscar Wilde—his parents forbade him from coming home because of the political and social unrest there. So he looked at the map of his dreams and the compass pointed him to the Pacific. That's how he ended up in Kristol.

"North Kristol?" I say.

"Think about it, Ken Z." CaZZ pauses to do so, then, giving up, says, "If you're a tourist, or even a teacher looking for work on this island, where would you go first? The north, right?"

I nod. Mr. Oku's story is beginning to sound more like my mom's. Both were from different countries in search of a place to call *their* home. Both were tourists who ended up settling—and working—in North Kristol. I wonder if they had known each other or crossed paths there.

"So you both think Mr. Oku and his roommate met there?"

"Where else?" CaZZ nods. "Estelle and I suspect Jeff was in the military."

"Totally fit the full-metal-jacket profile," Estelle says. "Buzz cut. Stood with his back straight at all times, like any moment he was going to raise his hand in a salute."

"And he never made eye contact when he talked to us," CaZZ says. "Always looked straight ahead. Probably PTSD."

"Post-traumatic shell shock disorder," Estelle says, making up her own acronym.

"You two with your imaginations," I say. "You should collaborate on fan fiction. And, Estelle, the *S* in PTSD stands for stress."

"It's shell shock, Ken Z," Estelle insists. "No one goes to war and comes back stressed."

"That's probably why they moved to South Kristol—to get away from warmongers," CaZZ says.

"Well, *I* wonder if they found out about Jeff, because you can't be gay, or lesbian, and be in the military in North Kristol, right?" Estelle says.

"Are you sure Jeff was in the military?"

"Regardless, Ken Z," CaZZ says. "I'm almost certain it's not allowed there. No gay soldiers. No gay marriages. No gay rights, period. They might as well make homosexuality illegal there."

"That's why you seldom read about gays and lesbians in North Kristol on the Internet," Estelle says.

"You can't believe everything you read online, Estelle," I say, echoing Ran's words.

"Please, Ken Z, there are hardly any articles about LGBTQs," CaZZ says. "It's almost as if they don't exist there."

"Not like here," Estelle continues. "Fucked up as it is, at least there are laws here that protect gays and lesbians from discrimination."

"For now, anyway," CaZZ adds. "But over there, who knows what they do to homosexuals."

"Probably send them to war, like they do to their prisoners,"

I want to say, but then they will want to know where I got such an idea from, and, because I'm not good enough of a liar, I will end up spilling the beans and breaking my promise to Ran.

"At least this place is a little more open to all sorts of people," Estelle says.

"I take this fucked-up, corrupt, hopeless, useless, gone-to-the-dogs-but-still-open-to-queens-and-queers, third-world-with-a-fourth-world-sewage-system-of-a-place over that prison of a paradise any day," CaZZ says.

"For now, anyway," Estelle says.

"Yes," CaZZ says. "For now, anyway."

Just then, the phone in my backpack vibrates. I hope it's a Zap from Ran and not my mom. I want to unzip my bag and kill the suspense now. But CaZZ and Estelle are eyeing me suspiciously. They must've seen the look on my face go from blah to bliss, which I cannot relish, not even for a minute. Estelle has a huge grin on her face. And CaZZ is giving me a look of reminder that in a true friendship, secrets are not meant for keeping but sharing.

Estelle, with her chin, points to the phone. "Ken Zap, are you going to answer it?"

CaZZ chimes in. "Yeah, Ken Z, answer it."

"Nah," I say, trying to sound nonchalant. "It's only my mom."

"Of course it is," CaZZ says, challenging my lie with hers. "Who else could it be? Right, Estelle?"

"Right."

"Ken Z." CaZZ smiles. Then, in that playful tone she uses when she wants to pry open my Pandora's box, she asks: "What happened during spring break?"

128

"Nothing." And to convince them, and myself, that I am getting better at lying, I say, with a stronger dose of confidence, that I spent the spring break at home, reading Oscar Wilde, watching DVDs, and eating pizzas.

"I see."

"Why?" I ask.

"Nothing," CaZZ says. "It's just that you're glowing—again."

"Whatever," I say.

I turn to Estelle. She is about to say something but instead gives me that wink with a mile-wide smile that tells me she can wait, that she doesn't mind waiting, until I'm good and ready to tell her why, at the vibrating sound of my phone, my heart almost jumped out of my chest and knocked her in the face.

End of interrogation.

Whew.

SENT WEDNESDAY 3/13, 5:15 P.M.

Ken Zapped!
Crazy-busy.
Save me Friday.

SENT WEDNESDAY 3/13, 5:38 P.M.

Whowhowhowhowhow?????

SENT WEDNESDAY 3/13, 5:40 P.M.

That's a WHO, by the way.

SENT WEDNESDAY 3/13, 5:43 P.M.

BTW, you still owe me a haiku.
And now a secret.
Shhh. CaZZ might hear us.

Sent Wednesday 3/13, 5:38 P.M.
CAZZ
Ken ZZZZZZZ, I'm so excited. . . .

Sent Wednesday 3/13, 5:39 P.M.
CAZZ
For you!

Sent Wednesday 3/13, 5:39 P.M.
CAZZ
Share ASAP K?
Promise I won't tell
Big-Mouth Estelle.

EVENING BLOSSOMS

Wednesday whispers,
My secret blossoms await
To sweeten nightfall.

Big Mouth Strikes Almost

Thursday, 14 March

This afternoon, I almost gave the secret away. I couldn't hide my excitement. It's the one thing I've been waiting for all week long—a Zap from Ran, his first since we parted last Sunday. The fact that he Zapped proves I'm still on his mind. Regardless, I have to learn to hide my happiness better. No matter how much I want to share it with CaZZ and Estelle, I made a promise to Ran. I can't—and won't—break it, even if the secret is getting heavier and heavier to lug around. I just can't. It would be like breaking a spell and bringing a hasty end to this story that's barely just begun.

LOVE & OTHER SADNESS

It's sad.

To love.

Love.

And hide.

The Ides of Yikes

FRIDAY EVENING, 15 MARCH. KEN Z'S BEDROOM.

OSCAR: Feeling all right, Ken Z?

ME: Honestly, Oscar? N. O.

OSCAR: What's the matter? Aren't you excited? All you did all day was stroll among the clouds.

ME: I don't think he's going to show up.

OSCAR: But that's not possible. Maybe he's just late. Again.

ME: That's an understatement.

OSCAR: What is it with people in North Kristol and their lateness?

ME: You'd think they'd be more punctual, right?

OSCAR: Well, it is a Friday. The tunnel is probably congested.

ME: True. Still, that's no excuse.

OSCAR: I say you give him one demerit when he shows up.

ME: Make that two.

OSCAR: Yes, laugh it off. That's the spirit.

ME: This whole thing is getting weirder and weirder. I haven't seen him in five days. You'd think the feeling would diminish by now—

OSCAR: But?

ME: But it's still there, following me around like an extra shadow.

OSCAR: He must be very special to you, Ken Z.

ME: Just not sure if he feels the same.

OSCAR: I beg your pardon?

ME: One Zap out of the week, Oscar, compared to my thirty thousand?

OSCAR: Dear child, don't reduce your feelings to numbers. And stop analyzing the future. Let it happen. Leave room for surprises.

ME: How?

OSCAR: By being your charming self. The Ken Z that he met and adored.

ME: Be myself?

OSCAR: You have no choice, dear boy. Everyone else is already taken.

The Song of Silence

I am a body of questions rushing to greet him at the door. And before I can utter a word, he puts a finger to my lips and smiles. He's not having any tonight. Words. He takes me by the hand and quietly guides me in as if we're sneaking into my apartment. And there, in my room with its wastebasket brimming with failed lists and poems, the mime continues. He pulls out a disc from inside his charcoal-gray jacket, the kind I see athletes wear in our schools, then tosses it onto my bed. I'm about to ask about the disc when he flags me down with a hand. CD player on, he walks me to the center of my room. The song begins. I don't know it, but I recognize the voice immediately. My eyes widen. He hushes my surprise. We stand there, listening to the first words of the night delivered to us by the crystal clear voice of Ella Fitzgerald. "He's a fool and don't I know it," she says, matter-of-factly. "But a fool can have his charm." And before I know it, he and I are holding hands, swaying, our bodies almost touching. I'm smiling because he's smiling, the two of us dancing in the middle of our small universe, while Ella continues to serenade us with a song that seems to sum up my thoughts and feelings these past two weeks. *Charms. Wild. Beguiled.* With my hand firmly gloved in his, he places them on his chest, and we sway some more. He releases his hold only when he feels my hand aching to open up, spread its fingers, like a web over his heart. *A simpering, whimpering child again.* And when he catches me stealing a glance at him, he wraps his arms around me, and I become bewildered again. This is what happens when one opens one's self up to the person that they like—grace and warmth come rushing forth all at once. He gives me a wink of a smile and leads our dancing bodies toward that perfect sway, and the moment my head touches his shoulder and he tightens his embrace, all those hours of worrying, those crumpled balls of paper wanting to be a perfect list, those sleepless nights tossing and turning, all those sad moments and doubts melt away.

IMAGINING THE DIVINE

On the divan, Ran
Looking like Dorian Gray
His scarlet lips pursed.

Frienniversary

Saturday, 16 March

Today marked the second-week anniversary of our friendship. To celebrate our frienniversary, he surprised me by driving me to Mirage. That's Ran. Full of surprises. Like this morning, when he showed up at my front door unannounced. Luckily, my mom had just left for work. I cannot even begin to imagine how the scene would've played out if she had answered the door.

As we approached the mall, I made a comment about looking forward to eating an overpriced free-range-chicken wrap again. It was meant as sarcasm, a joke. But it was where we ended up— Buddha's Joint, where our story began.

On the way to the restaurant, we passed a young guy who would've stood out in a packed stadium. He was dressed up like he was time-traveling from the Victorian era of Oscar Wilde. He could've easily passed for one of Oscar's artsy-fartsy friends. Thin and flamboyant in a dandyish way, he had on a black bowler hat, pin-striped pants, pointy shoes, a ruffled shirt, and a yellow kerchief tucked into the breast pocket of his coat.

I was about to point him out to Ran when I noticed that they were already exchanging knowing glances with sly grins on their faces. The guy winked at Ran; Ran winked back. I felt the sharp tooth of the green-eyed monster dig into me. I'd never felt this sort of jealousy before. It was deep. It made me feel small, insignificant, like South Kristol. It made me so insecure and ugly—this gross feeling that I can easily be replaced.

"You know that guy, Ran?" I asked, as casually as possible so he wouldn't detect my jealousy.

Ran, still smiling, nodded. "He's *a she*."

"A she?" I tried to suppress my sudden elation. It wasn't easy; inside me was a gospel choir shouting "Hallelujah!"

I didn't believe him. I turned back to look at her, hunt for traces of a girl hiding behind the clothes. None. She was flamboyantly dressed, yet boyish-looking.

"She's only in tenth grade—and already a pro," he said.

"A pro?"

"At bunburying."

"No way."

"She deceived you, right?"

"Yes," I said, laughing. She reminded me of Estelle, except Estelle doesn't need clothes to muddle people's idea of boys and girls.

Then it hit me—again!—this feeling that I've been suppressing since day one: the hunch that Ran was a bunburyist who was—and still is—bunburying me. Is this why he seldom Zaps? Is this why he's always full of surprises? But if he's bunburying, then as what? Ken Z's secret friend?

I stopped myself.

What was I doing? Ruining our frienniversary. Stinking the moment with rubbish thoughts. So I trashed them. But not without hesitation.

Rough Draft for Eternity

Sunday, 17 March

Ran picks up a sheet of paper on my desk. A smile widens on his face as he reads the list. Then he starts humming the Cole Porter tune. "This is about De-Us, right?"

I pretend to not know what he's talking about. But it's difficult to keep a poker face when he's holding a piece of paper with my heart spilled all over it.

"It *is* about us," he continues.

I want to lie and tell him no. I don't want him—or anyone—to know I write about us. It's personal, not meant to be shared, even with the guy who inspired it. Besides, it's not finished, and I'm very superstitious about sharing anything that's still in progress. I'm afraid I'll never be able to finish it if I do. I have to figure it out first, I have to be part of its world, live in it. Otherwise, it won't ring true. Otherwise, it won't be fun building it.

"You a writer, Ken Z?"

"No. I just like making lists," I say. "Force of habit."

"Then you're a writer!" he exclaims.

I don't respond, so he pushes the issue.

"Can I have it when you're done?"

Without waiting for an answer, he says, "And I want it signed by the author." He checks his watch. "It's goodbye time again, Ken Z." He makes an exaggerated sad face with his lower lip jutting out. "Goodbyes suck. Royally."

I rise from the chair, and as I pass him, he grabs my hand. "Not so fast, mister."

I struggle to loosen his grasp.

"What's wrong?" He grips my wrist, forcing me to look him in the eye.

I shrug.

Finally, the words roll out of me. "Ran, did you ever get my Zaps?"

"I did. And I Zapped back."

"Yeah, once," I say. "How come?"

"I couldn't," he says.

"Why?"

It's his turn to shrug. "It's not that easy, Ken Z."

"What do you mean?"

"Let's not talk about it, okay?" To put the issue to rest, he pulls me toward him, hugs me so tightly I can barely breathe. He leans closer, his lips almost touching mine. I open my mouth to meet his.

Then I withdraw.

Because he withdrew.

It's not a kiss he wants but to rest his head on my shoulder.

We stand there, embracing each other for what seems like forever and a half, his breath warm and heavy on my neck. Next thing I know, I'm kissing him. Because he's kissing me. Ravenously.

As if the world is coming to an end.

And if it is, it's the perfect finale.
It feels nice and comforting.
To be held like that.
And wanted.
And reassured.

Hopelessly Writing

Monday night, 18 March

Checked my phone again. No Zaps. Not tonight. It's already nine p.m. Why do I even bother? It's Monday, first day of school week. It means he's crazy-busy. It means I can Zap but shouldn't expect a reply. . . . He's probably asleep, while I continue to fill the pages of this journal with ~~redundant questions longing~~ urgent matters. Stop. Breathe. Reboot. Then try to form a thought without Ran in it, like . . . coming up with a list of possible names for the book club.

In the beginning, I didn't see the point of having one. Neither did the others—Estelle, Matt, and Tanya—especially since graduation is two months away. But CaZZ, whom we unanimously elected president, insisted on it. "We can't have a legacy without a name," she said. "We're the ones who started it, so it is our right and responsibility to christen it. It will make our book club official. But it has to be a name that's witty, you know, catchy, a title Oscar Wilde would approve of."

So, come tomorrow, we will meet after school to christen our book club. I'm actually looking forward to it; it's our first get-together since spring break. I can't wait to hear more of Matt (mis)quoting Oscar. "The only way to get rid of temptation is to pray to it" (as opposed to "yield to it") and "Be yourself. Nobody else wants it" instead of "because everyone else is already taken." Estelle finds his errors hilarious. I do, too. But they irk the hell out of CaZZ and Tanya, a bottom-of-the-pyramid cheerleader who joined the book club to maintain her C average.

Starting to get sleepy. Writing is exhausting, especially if it's about something I don't want to forget. Writing is a way of saving memories, of not letting go. I guess that's why I write. I don't know how else to save something precious. I don't know how else to let go. Worse-case scenario: I could be doing something more exhausting, like waiting for the number eight bus. Or for Ran to Zap me.

Oscar's Wilde Tribe Presents "The Importance of Being Nameless": Our Book Club

In One Act (Thank God!)

THE PLAYERS

CaZZ—President, voted unanimously because nobody, except her, wanted to be it.

Estelle—Vice President, voted unanimously because nobody else, not even her, wanted to be it.

Me Z—Secretary, voted unanimously because nobody else, except for me, can touch-type.

Matt—Treasurer. A born-again jock, though we're convinced he's a closeted atheist.

Tanya—Mascot (still to be decided by the club). *The Picture of Dorian Gray,* she admitted, was the only novel that she'd read, including the introduction by a literary critic that none of us bothered to read. She also confessed that her ideal boyfriend is someone like Dorian Gray ("Even if he's fictional!"). Even after we reminded her that Dorian drove his girlfriend to commit suicide.

Mr. Oku—Twelfth-grade literature teacher and advisor of our book club devoted to the writings of Oscar Wilde.

Time: Tuesday, 19 March. After school.

Place: South Kristol High School. Bldg. H-204. Mr. Oku's classroom.

TANYA: I got it. How about "The Dorian Grays"?

MATT: Too gay.

TANYA: And Oscar wasn't?

MATT: I don't think Oscar was gay. He was married and had two sons. Maybe he was bi or on the DL.

CAZZ: I don't think a guy on the down-low would parade around dressed up like a dandy, and especially not with a green carnation on his fur-lined coat.

TANYA: Means nothing nowadays, anyway.

MATT: But back then it did. How else would you prove you weren't "gay"? Right, Mr. Oku?

MR. OKU: Matt's got a point. However, "gay" as we know it today did not mean the same thing as during Oscar's time.

CAZZ: Just like the word *faggot*.

ME: Which was a bundle of twigs used to burn witches.

TANYA: I swear, Ken Z, you make Quikiepedia look retarded.

MATT: Wait. So Oscar Wilde didn't go to prison because he was gay?

MR. OKU: No. He was found guilty of engaging in sex with men, referred to during the Victorian era as an act of "gross indecency."

MATT: Sounds so *1984*.

CAZZ: I got one. Kind of long, though. "Oscar Wilde's Reading Group Therapy for the Battered Colonized Renegades."

ESTELLE: Wow, CaZZ, we'll be eighty and attached to urine bags by the time we're done saying it.

CAZZ: True that.

149

TANYA: How about "A Book Club of No Importance of Being a Book Club"?

MATT: I kind of like that, Tanya. Very elliptical.

TANYA: Thanks, Matt. Took me almost forever to think of it.

ESTELLE: How about "The Bunburyists"?

MR. OKU: Good one, Estelle.

ME: Yeah, brilliant.

TANYA: Love it. But too deceiving, no?

CAZZ: Hello? Isn't that the point of bunburying?

TANYA: Okay, then, if we are a book club in the city, what are we in the countryside?

CAZZ: Matt's Gospel Choir?

ME: I like it. It's catchy. Oscar Witty.

MATT: Too earnest.

ME: That's it.

MATT: What?

ME: The Earnest Book Club.

TANYA: As in Bert and Ernie's Book Club?

CAZZ: No, Einstein. Earnest. E-A-R-N-E-S-T. Right, Ken Z?

ME: Yeah. But E-R-N works too.

CAZZ: I like E-A-R-N.

MR. OKU: Good one, Ken Z.

ESTELLE: Mucho gustorilla.

CAZZ: The Earnest Book Club. Witty.

TANYA: And punny.

MR. OKU: Okay. Time to vote.

TANYA: Are you voting too?

MR. OKU: No, Tanya. Just you five.

ESTELLE: I personally like the Earnest Book Club.

CAZZ: Me too.

ME: I like the Bunburyists.

MATT: Same.

CAZZ: Tanya.

TANYA: I vote for the Bunburyists. No . . . wait . . . the Earnest Book Club.

ESTELLE: *Dépêchez*-twat.

TANYA: Okay. The Earnest Book Club.

CAZZ: Is that your final decision?

TANYA: Yup.

CAZZ: Are you sure?

MATT: Take it, before she changes her mind.

CAZZ: The Wilde tribe has spoken. From here on, we are officially the Earnest Book Club.

(Burst of applause and cheers)

UNREQUITED ZAP #44

SENT TUESDAY 3/19, 4:28 P.M.

Ran, we're no longer
Nameless. Call us The Earnest
Book Club. Zap soon. K

The Stupidest Thing

Wednesday, 20 March

Barely slept last night. Had a difficult time going back to sleep after the nightmare. In the dream, I was on the phone with Ran but we kept getting cut off by a man talking gibberish, his voice getting louder and angrier. Not sure what that means. Dreams are supposed to be symbolic, metaphorical, not to be interpreted literally. But I did, and today, after I got home from school, I waited for Ran's Zap all afternoon and into the evening because today is Wednesday and the only time he Zapped me last week was on a Wednesday, at around 4:30 p.m. while CaZZ and Estelle were filling me in on their camping trip. So I waited for his Zap. Four-thirty p.m. turned into 5, then into 6, 7, 8, 9. Unable to wait any longer, I did the stupidest thing and finally phoned him, which had never crossed my mind before because he made me promise never to call him. I thought I heard someone on the other line. The voice sounded computerized. "We are unable to come to the phone right now," it said, "so leave us a brief message and we'll get back to you." Then I heard a female voice in the background. She sounded mad, angry, as if she were scolding someone (Ran?). Her voice grew louder and louder, until it felt like she was screaming in my ears, telling me to hang up or else . . . or else. . . .

The Difficult List

It's difficult to be a geek in love.
I split the hour between waiting and getting frustrated,
   between longing and worrying,
   between tossing and hoping.
It's difficult to keep him away from my thoughts.
Worse when I'm writing a list or a haiku;
   I can't count syllables past his smiling face.
It's difficult having a conversation with him;
   he's got a way of holding me hostage
   with his steel-gray gaze.
More difficult when he's holding my hand.
I have to pray for my palms to stay dry,
   my heart to keep still.
It's difficult when he tells me to keep our rendezvous
   a secret from my friends
   who can read between the lies.
It's difficult to play dumb when I'm cowriting the story.
It's difficult when he lives there and I live here
   and he wants to communicate only via Zap.
Even more difficult when he Zaps me only once a week.

Compared to my gazillions to him.
It's difficult to love a love that's different,
that most people don't understand,
or don't want to.
And because they don't understand, they hate it
with such passion.
In some countries, it's against the law.
In others, it's punishable by death.
Oscar Wilde was sentenced to prison
because of such love.
It's difficult to be in love.
Plain and simple.
Love is rarely plain.
And never simple.

Difficult now to imagine this world without him.

THURSDAY'S FORECAST

Outside my window
He's there, dancing in my thoughts—
Hazy day ahead.

Ode to Errors

FRIDAY AFTERNOON, 22 MARCH. MY BEDROOM.

OSCAR: Making a list, are we?

ME: Trying to. But as you can see, the only thing I've accomplished so far are these balls of crumpled paper.

OSCAR: Remember, dear heart, every masterpiece is born from *The Book of False Starts*. Beneath the *Mona Lisa* are layers and layers of paint from thousands and thousands of brushstrokes. *(Pauses.)* Have patience, Ken Z, you'll get there. Eventually.

ME: Can eventually be tonight?

OSCAR *(laughs)*: There's no way of telling. The process is all very mysterious; only critics have managed to fathom it, as they pride themselves in knowing more about Art than the artists who toil over their craft day and night.

ME: So I shouldn't rush the head rush?

OSCAR: Exactly.

ME: I just want it to be, you know—

OSCAR: De-vine?

ME: Perfect.

OSCAR: Perfect?

ME: Yes.

OSCAR: My dear boy, leave Perfection—stepfather of Spontaneity and Fun—to critics and their audience. Besides, you already know that a list is never-ending. Its roots and branches keep growing and growing. Like a tree that thinks of itself as both sky and sea.

ME: Endlessness.

OSCAR: Yes. So be the tree that roams among the clouds and dives with the dolphins. What matters is the dedication you put into your list. Weigh each word carefully, as if the Earth needs it to orbit around the sun. And . . .

ME: Yes?

OSCAR: Don't be afraid to make mistakes, Ken Z. Decorate the Room of Grand Ideas with errors. Be patient. Don't rush the head rush. Enjoy the joyride. And above all, open thyself to the mystery. The creative process is an amazing affair. The end result can lead to nothing—a void, a wrong turn, a false start. Or it can be the most magnificent mistake you will make thus far. Now sleep, my child, and let your dreams continue the list for you.

ME: Thanks, Oscar.

OSCAR: Mention not, dear child. Mention not.

Ditched

Friday, 22 March. 5:00 p.m.

I committed the unspeakable. I backed out of my movie date with CaZZ and Estelle. I couldn't say no to them in person. They would've cornered me, fired questions until the truth shook out of me. I waited till I got home and broke the news to them. I made up some excuse about having eaten something spoiled. I feel ~~bad~~ gross about lying. I don't know why I'm still hiding Ran from them. They're so intuitive it's frightening.

CaZZ was the first to Zap back. "Yeah, right, whatever, Ken Z." Estelle's message stung more. "YOU never ever said NO to a movie. EVER!" If she was guilt-tripping me, she succeeded. It feels as if I've just been pushed to the ground, with my tongue licking the dirt.

They've got every right to be pissed. This is the first time in the history of our friendship that I was not going to the movies with them.

But I had no choice. Today's Friday. It's my and Ran's day. I haven't seen him in five days. The weekends are our only chance to hang out—tonight, tomorrow, and, maybe, if time

161

permits, Sunday, which is a big MAYBE. Every minute counts with him.

Besides, I can't just leave the house. Ran has a bad habit of showing up at the front door unannounced. I can't even go to the corner store, for fear that I'll miss him. I want to be here to open the door, to laugh at the sight of him holding a large pizza and a bottle of Fanta Orange.

I need to be here when he knocks. He's not the type to hang around my front door. I don't think he's ever had to wait for anyone in his life. With us, it's always been me who did the waiting. I can't even doze off because if I do and I don't hear his knocking, then what?

Ran, please show up. I ditched my friends for you. Please give my lie some validity.

INVISIBLE #1

It's almost midnight.
No magic spell at the door.
Happiness on hold.

Acceptance/Rejection

Saturday, 23 March. 5:00 p.m.

Stayed home all day in my room. No sign of Ran. Still early. I'll let the worrying game begin at 6.

I should shoot him another Zap. In case . . . in case what? So he knows how much time I waste thinking wondering wanting. This is absurd crazy unreal real.

There are other things worth losing sleep over, like . . . opening the pile of acceptance—or rejection—letters on my desk from colleges and universities promising what I already know. That a better life is waiting for me outside of South Kristol, a place that the locals can be proud of, where they don't feel small or insignificant. Half of me says, "Stay, Ken Z, you don't need to leave South Kristol to make your mark." But the other half says, "Get out, Ken Z, listen to your mom, dreams here turn to rust."

. . .

I feel so URGHANIC right now. I can't think straight. All I can
see is a NOW that's shrinking because Ran is not in it. I better go
back to my list, clean it up. Who knows? Maybe he'll pop in by
the time I'm done. After all, it's a list about him.

I DON'T STAND A GHOST (OF A CHANCE)

A week of ghosting
Is our secret still valid?
My heart on ransom.

Fragments

I have not left the house since Friday. Not once. It's already Sunday. I feel like a prisoner in my own apartment. I don't have to be. I have the key to my cell and can easily walk out. Then what's stopping me? Stupid me. Crazy me. Wishful-thinking me. Hopelessly hopeful me.

Thinking of calling him up just to get it over and done with. What if his mother answers, or some eerie voice like that in the recording? What if he got into trouble because of me? What if this is why all weekend long it's been Me-Minus-Ran? Still, he could've Zapped to say so. How difficult is it to say, "Sorry, busy this weekend"? Or, "Ken Z, forget us, okay?"

Six hours left before hope dies.

· · ·

CaZZ and Estelle have not Zapped since I bowed out of our movie date. No Zap, no butt calls, no harassing me for a haiku. They're pissed off. I know; my ears are ringing. I'm already dreading the thought of seeing them tomorrow.

Is madness the other side of head rush?

Sucks. Royally.

Nonresponsive

Monday, 25 March

CaZZ and Estelle cornered me in the library today after school. Luckily there was a cartload of books to shelve and keep myself busy with while they took turns ganging up on me. I let them; I really wasn't in the mood for an argument with the wonder twins. I was still upset, very upset, about Ran ghosting me this weekend. About me keeping myself in prison all weekend. About not knowing if Ran's all right. About not knowing the status of our secret. About feeling hopeless and helpless. About having to lie to my friends. About the light at the end of my tunnel fading faster and faster.

"So what, Ken Z? Still got the runs?" CaZZ asked.

"What're you talking about?" I completely forgot about the little white lie I told them. By the time I remembered, it was too late. CaZZ and Estelle were already on a roll spelling it out for me.

"You know, the runs that made you skip out on our movie date."

The word GUILTY flashed across my forehead in bold letters,

but I maintained my silence, afraid that if I said something I would regret it later. Sometimes no reaction is more effective.

"Got the *runs*? Call Dr. Ken Z for a free consultation," Estelle chimed in.

Then CaZZ broke out into an oldie-but-goodie. "I want to run to you, ooooooh."

Not wanting to be beaten, Estelle jumped in with "Da doo ron ron ron, da doo ron ron."

A knee-jerk reaction because I thought I heard Ran's name. I was about to break my silence and tell them both to shut up when CaZZ started singing, "Lo-o-ving you is easy 'cause you're byoo-tee-fu-u-ull."

Then she and Estelle cracked their voices reaching for the high notes; they sounded like a pair of mynah birds being choked to death.

On an ordinary day, I would've laughed. But today was far from ordinary. I don't recall having an ordinary day since I met Ran; it's either been extraordinarily amazing or a fingernails-clawing-across-the-blackboard day. All I wanted was to finish shelving the books, then go home and lock myself in my room.

My indifference must've tired them out, because they soon gave up. "Okay, Ken Z, show's over," Estelle said. "We love you too much to waste our angelic voices on you."

"So what did you do Friday?" CaZZ asked.

"Who did you trade our movie date for?" Estelle butted in.

"Already told you. I stayed home."

"Alone?" CaZZ asked.

I threw an invisible dagger at CaZZ.

CaZZ backed off. "Whew, Estelle, did you see that? Ken Z just gave me the evil eye."

"Don't know what you're talking about, CaZZ," Estelle remarked. I caught her winking at me, which was all I needed for the load of a heavy day to lighten. It's amazing how one gesture like a wink or a smile is sometimes enough to make us forget our crazy situation for a moment.

"Let's go, CaZZ," Estelle said. "I think Ken Z's had enough of us for the day."

"You're right, Estelle," she said, "absolutely right."

They left, but not without Estelle throwing me another wink. "Cheer up, Ken Z," she seemed to be saying. "Whatever it is, dude, it will pass."

MONDAY'S BARGAINING

The list is finished.
Autographed and all. So come
Help me shave my head.

Heart-Stopping Things He Says

"Be random with me."

"Even if I twist your arm—gently?"

"It's not an Oscar Wilde fairy tale if beauty doesn't come with pain."

"It's de-ran-duran!"

"More like 'Ran over.'"

"Sucks. Royally."

"It's Latin for 'from the depths.'"

"Like a ghost playing with your mind."

"You and I can be a pair of Buddhist monks."

"It's de-ken-ken dance."

"Can you reboot?"

"It's de-ken-ta-loupe."

"Transmission is a little choppy."

"Traffic inferno."

"It's de-doop-du-jour."

"You keep breaking up, Ken Zarooni."

"Ever go beyond seventeen syllables?"

"See us tomorrow."

The Last of Us

Tuesday, 26 March

Tossed and turned all night, trying to remember if Ran and I officially made plans to see each other this past weekend. Did he actually say, "See us this weekend, Ken Z?" Or did I just dream up those words?

Over and over, I replay in my head the last time we saw each other. It was two Sundays ago. We were in my room, talking about how much we hate goodbyes. Then I asked him why he only Zapped me once. He told me he couldn't, then threw his arms around me to shut me up.

But did we make any specific plans? I'm not sure anymore, though he did say he was going to keep seeing me until I got tired of him. I know; I remember; I wrote it down. I don't let words like that get away from me. They mean too much. Like that lingering hug he gave me before walking away.

. . .

He didn't want to leave. I could tell by the way he looked at me, like he was afraid that once he disappeared down the corridor, I wouldn't be there when he looked back.

That is my last memory of us.

Sometimes all it takes is a nervous twitch,
a smile knocking on the front door,
an accidental brush of his arm against yours
for the memory to begin breathing again.

DAWN

Not quite morning
Not quite wakefulness—
My craving crows.

SENT FRIDAY 3/29, 5:30 A.M.

Hey stranger, you k?
Are we on for tonight? Zap
Back. Just me, Ken Z.

Happily Never After

Friday, 29 March. South Kristol High School. Bldg. H-204.
Mr. Oku's classroom.

"They're so heartbreaking," Estelle says of Oscar's fairy tales.

"Yet so beautiful," CaZZ says.

"Very," I say, remembering what Ran said—that it's not an Oscar Wilde fairy tale if beauty does not come with pain.

"Talk about Debbie Downer," Tanya says. "They're so depressing, but so addictive too. I couldn't put them down."

"Me too," Matt says. He was at a Christian youth camp for spring break and read the fairy tales between Bible study groups.

"I spent the entire break crying," Tanya says. "The stories made me so sad I had to see my therapist afterward."

"I had to talk to my pastor," says Matt.

"About what?" I ask.

"About martyrdom," he answers.

"They're so violent," Estelle says. "I love it. It's like watching an anime. I especially love that scene where the nightingale stabs her heart again and again with the thorn of a white rose. I can't get the image out of my head."

"And the swallow plucking out the sapphire eyes of the happy prince statue, then peeling his gold skin until he's nothing but lead," I say.

"Ouch." Tanya flinches.

"Make that a double," Matt says. "Wonder what that says about me?"

I'm about to tell him that maybe Oscar's addicted to pain, but CaZZ beats me to it.

"That makes two of us," Tanya says.

"Girl, you were into pain before Oscar Wilde entered your life," CaZZ says, laughing.

"True." Tanya laughs too. "I'm still dating the same loser, going on three weeks now."

We all laugh. Even Mr. Oku, who sits behind his desk, watching and listening to us with amusement.

"But you know what?" Tanya continues. "I kept waiting for the 'happily ever after' part and it never came. What kind of fairy tale is that?"

"Happily never after," I answer. Estelle detects my sarcasm and wink-smiles at me.

"Are these even fairy tales, Mr. Oku?" Tanya asks.

"No, Tanya," CaZZ retorts, "they're memoirs with sacrificial birds and talking statues."

"What's your favorite fairy tale?" Tanya asks her.

And CaZZ answers, "Hands down 'The Devoted Friend.'" Pause. "Because it's about the unselfishness of true friendship." She points her eyes at me, waiting to see whether or not I'll react. I don't, so she tries to provoke me some more. "I think anyone who's ever had a friend like the greedy, self-absorbed, unreliable, undependable Big Hugh knows the kind of friend I'm talking about."

I ignore her remark.

"Tell me about it," Tanya blurts out. "The cheerleading squad is full of backstabbing competitive bitches. We all pretend we're best of friends when we're actually the worst of enemies."

Estelle nods. "We call people like those 'abuser-friendly.'"

"Well, does Little Hans even know he's being used?" I ask. "I don't think so. He keeps giving and giving until he ends up with nothing. He's so naive, so ignorant that everyone takes advantage of him. Like Big Hugh sending him on errands at ungodly hours, or bombarding him with favors, or never leaving him alone so he can tend to his garden."

"That's because Little Hans is blind as a bat," Tanya says, "and people like him become perfect victims for assholes like Big Hugh."

"Speaking from experience, Tanya?" CaZZ says.

"Damn right, CaZZ."

"I don't think there's anything wrong with naivete," Matt says. "I mean, what's ignorance to you, Ken Z, is *innocence* to others. That's what makes Little Hans so admirable and special in the first place."

"Good point, Matt," Estelle says.

"Would you rather be naive, like Little Hans, or corrupt and deceptive, like Big Hugh?" Matt asks.

"Neither," I reply.

"It's one or the other, Ken Z," CaZZ says.

"Those choices are so limiting," I say. "Besides, I don't think that's the point Oscar is trying to convey."

"Really?" CaZZ says, sarcastically.

"Yes," I say. "I think Oscar is trying to show us the thin line between devotion and stupidity."

"Want to expound on that more, Ken Z?" Mr. Oku says.

"If Little Hans were less ignorant and more assertive, then, maybe, he could've saved himself from death."

"At least his funeral was packed," Tanya says.

I'm about to say something when CaZZ says, "Little Hans has low self-esteem, Ken Z. That's why he can't be assertive."

Estelle takes over. "You're right, CaZZ. Little Hans doesn't know how wonderful he is. He's always downplaying himself, always thinking he's never good enough, that his ideas will never be as beautiful as Big Hugh's."

I am speechless. Estelle's and CaZZ's words sting. It's obvious they are talking about me, telling me to my face that besides being ignorant and naive, I also have low self-esteem and don't know just how special I am.

"In fact, Little Hans is as perfect a friend as anybody can have," Estelle says. "Right, CaZZ?"

"Absolutely," CaZZ says.

"If I could be one of the characters in Oscar's fairy tales, I'd choose Little Hans," Matt says. "What about you, Estelle?"

"That's a tough one," Estelle replies. "They all die—"

"Violently," CaZZ interjects.

Estelle nods in agreement. "That's almost like asking me how I want to die violently," she says. "Let's see. Do I want to be skinned to death like the Happy Prince?"

"Or drown like Little Hans?" CaZZ says.

"Or bleed to death like the nightingale?" Tanya suggests.

"I guess I'd rather go like the selfish giant," Estelle says.

"Why?" Tanya asks. "He just drops dead. How boring is that?"

"True," Estelle says. "But at least he was able to make peace with the children and die a beautiful, yet uneventful death." Pause. "What about you, Ken Z?"

I sit on Estelle's question for a moment. "The Nightingale and the Rose" is my favorite, hands down. I can never forget the image of the nightingale impaling its heart on the thorn of the rose, deeper and deeper, while it serenades the night with its song. But I end up going with "The Happy Prince."

"Interesting, Ken Z," Mr. Oku says. "Why is that?"

"We could use a couple of happy prince statues in South Kristol," I say. "Feed the poor. Shelter the homeless."

"Then we won't need aid from North Kristol," CaZZ says.

"And, maybe, just maybe, South Kristol can rise from its ashes like a phoenix and make this place like it was during the olden days, when the native Pulas were the only ones on the island," Estelle says.

"True," Tanya says. "After all, this entire island was theirs first."

"Before it was stolen from us," CaZZ says.

"How can the Pula natives govern if they can't even get along with each other?" Matt asks. "They tried, remember? But they only ended up killing each other."

Sadly, Matt's right. But what Matt is forgetting is that it was in the Pula blood to be a warrior. The race was divided into warring tribes, and regardless of which chiefdom one belonged to, a Pula was born a warrior, which means he was born to kill—or be killed.

"True," CaZZ says. "But we didn't kill as many as those killed

185

by the white man." Pause. "Besides, Matt, it's our land, it's our kingdom, however divided we were. And should we reclaim this island, how we plan to govern ourselves is up to us—not you or anybody else."

"Highly unlikely," Matt says. "Let's be practical, CaZZ. With all the wars happening around us, South Kristol cannot protect itself from foreign invasion without the help of North Kristol. If not for them protecting us, we'd probably be in worse shape right now."

"True," Tanya says.

"Hello?" Estelle chimes in. "The invasion of the North Kristol snatchers!"

"We're practically prisoners in our own home," CaZZ says. "Every move we make is recorded by surveillance cameras."

"True that," Tanya says.

"Those cameras are for our safety," Matt argues. "Crime has gone down because of them."

"True that too," Tanya interjects.

"Those are *their* cameras, Matt," CaZZ says. "They're probably monitoring us from the other side of the mountain."

The cameras! I've forgotten about the cameras. What if they recorded Ran and me? What if that's the reason why Ran's stopped Zapping me? Oh no. Calm down, Ken Z. We didn't do anything bad. Calm the heck down.

"Welcome to South Kristol, Big Brother," Estelle says.

"Except scarier," CaZZ adds.

"Pretty soon, they'll be controlling us," Tanya says.

"Hello?" CaZZ says. "They already are."

A dark cloud of silence hangs over our heads. Mr. Oku sweeps it away by telling us not to lose hope.

I raise my hand.

"Yes, Ken Z?"

"How did you end up here, Mr. Oku?" I ask.

He thinks out loud. "Let's see. How do I simplify this? After I got my degree from Oxford, I couldn't go home because a civil war had broken out there. I also didn't feel like staying in England, so I decided to travel. I didn't know where to. Then, one day, while I was perusing a travel magazine, I came across an ad promoting Kristol as the 'New Paradise of the Pacific.'"

"You mean North Kristol?" I ask.

Mr. Oku nods.

"So you came here as a tourist?" Tanya asks.

"Duh," CaZZ says.

"North Kristol was second only to Hawaii as the most popular tourist destination in the Pacific. It was also deemed one of the safest in the world."

"How can it not be?" CaZZ says. "Practically everyone there is wearing fatigues and toting a machine gun."

"NKRA mania!" Estelle says. North Kristol Rifle Association.

"I heard about their army, but I wasn't expecting the entire island to be one huge military base," Mr. Oku says. "This was before the Internet, and the tourism brochures did not focus on the military. So you can more or less imagine my shock when I got off the plane. Bases everywhere. Soldiers on the streets, inside the malls, on the beaches. There were cops, but the majority were soldiers. I'd never seen so many in my life. One cannot set foot in a mall, or even a fast-food joint, or go hiking without running into them. It was as if I were vacationing in Army paradise. The irony, of course, is that I did feel safe. And the beaches, waterfalls, and botanical gardens were simply majestic."

"But you stayed?" I ask.

"I didn't plan on it," Mr. Oku answers. "I couldn't go home. To top it off, the cost of living was still affordable, unlike now. It also just so happened that they were recruiting teachers. The salary was too good to turn down. I applied and, well, the rest, as they say, is history."

"Maybe we'll have a major makeover here soon," Tanya says.

"Don't worry, Tanya, it'll happen," CaZZ says. "This is just the foundation. When the makeup's done, it'll be just like Dorian Gray. Beautiful on the outside, but rotting and evil on the inside."

"How depressing," Tanya says. "Why can't life be depressing, yet beautiful, too, like an Oscar Wilde fairy tale? Why does it have to be depressing *and* ugly?"

"There's your happily ever after, Tanya," I say. "Depressing and painful, but beautiful."

"Can someone explain to me the point of 'The Nightingale and the Rose,' because I don't get it," Matt says. "Did the nightingale sacrifice her life for nothing?"

"There is no point," I remark. "If there is, it's 'Don't die for love, Matt, because, in the end, nobody gives a damn. Not even the person you're sacrificing your life for.'"

Estelle and CaZZ exchange WTH? looks. I don't need to be a mind reader to know what they're thinking. They heard me. I heard it, too; the bitterness in my voice that shot out of my mouth like bullets. Mr. Oku also heard it. It caught him so unexpectedly that he quickly sat up straight and turned to me. They all did.

Silence diffuses throughout the room, like poisonous gas. Thank God, Tanya disrupts the awkward moment by saying she

188

wishes Oscar Wilde came into her life sooner. "It would've saved me from pricks like Jerome and Leonard and Edmond."

"And your father's checking account—don't forget," Matt says, and laughs.

"I know." Tanya laughs along. "My love life is beyond anti-depressants. I hope the next Oscar Wilde book we're reading won't be as depressing as these fairy tales." She pauses and turns to Mr. Oku. "Is it?"

"Sadly, yes," Mr. Oku says. "We'll be reading *The Trials of Oscar Wilde*."

The depressing news excites us.

"Good morning, heartache!" CaZZ exclaims.

"Juicy Fruity," Estelle says.

"Totes," CaZZ says.

"Wow!" Matt remarks.

"The entire trial, Mr. Oku?" Tanya asks, sounding concerned.

Mr. Oku nods.

"Tanya's worried she might not be able to finish it before graduation, Mr. Oku," Estelle says.

"Is it thick?" Tanya asks.

"Don't worry, Tanya, it's a fast read," Mr. Oku says. "It's a transcript of the trials. It'll be like reading one of his plays."

"Faster than *The Importance of Being Earnest*?"

"So fast you'll feel like you were inside the courtroom."

"And watching your life go to pieces in two hours," CaZZ adds.

"Or less," I say, "if you speed-read."

Meeting adjourned.

I wait for everyone to leave the room. I pretend to be searching for my phone, my head practically inside my bag. CaZZ passes by me without a goodbye. Estelle, though, calls out my name. I poke my head out and see her gesturing me to call her. I wave a hand, give her a robotic nod.

"Ken Z, is everything all right?" Mr. Oku asks.

"Huh?" I say, feigning ignorance.

"Between you and CaZZ and Estelle," he says.

"Of course," I lie.

"That's good," he says, his lie more convincing than mine.

I'm about to step out the door when a nagging question stops me.

"Mr. Oku?"

"Yes?"

". . ." (Ask him, Ken Z, or bite your tongue forever.)

". . ." (Yes?)

"I don't mean to pry, but why did you leave North Kristol? I mean, if everything, as you said, was there—good salary, beautiful beaches, security—why trade all that to move here?"

Mr. Oku listens, nodding to every word I'm saying.

When I'm done asking, he raises his head. "I moved, Ken Z, because they changed the teaching curriculum," he says matter-of-factly. "They didn't want me teaching certain books to the students."

"Why?"

"They were afraid that the books would pollute the minds of the students."

"You mean like Oscar Wilde's books?"

He nods.

Then it's true, I tell myself, it's all true, about Ran's school, and his favorite English teacher who was fired from her job for letting him and other students read Oscar Wilde in secrecy because his books, among others, were—still are—banned in North Kristol. This explains why Ran's copy of *De Profundis* was covered in brown paper.

"So that's why you moved to South Kristol?" I ask.

"I don't see the purpose of teaching if I can't teach the books I love, Ken Z," Mr. Oku says. "It really is as simple as that. Books do not pollute minds if they can make you think about the world you live in, about yourself and your relationship with others. We become wiser, and, hopefully, better individuals because of literature. That is why I left North Kristol. Money can buy everything, Ken Z, except happiness and contentment."

His words leave me speechless. I've always respected and admired Mr. Oku. He's one of the more approachable teachers I've had. He makes reading literature exciting. After today, I respect and admire and appreciate him even more. He traded his first-class life for a third-world island nation, just so he can continue teaching the books deemed too dangerous for our minds. He chose happiness and contentment in our sad and small place, over security and wealth in the paradise of guns. If that's not wow, then I don't know what is.

ESTELLE'S ZAP

SENT FRIDAY 3/29, 6:00 P.M.

Ken Z, what's wrong, babe?
We're not mad at you, you know.
Answer my haiku.

Erased

I spent the whole day searching for whatever I could find about banned books in North Kristol. Nothing. *Strange,* I thought. Next, I tried "Oscar Wilde," "banned," and "North Kristol." Still no results. Then I typed "homosexuality" and "North Kristol" in the search engine. Several articles popped up. Nothing on same-sex marriage, but a few were on gays and lesbians in the military. As CaZZ and Estelle said, gays and lesbians are not allowed to serve in the military. If they're found out, they're given a dishonorable discharge, though not a single article mentioned punishment or imprisonment. Is homosexuality a crime there? Does one go to prison for being gay or lesbian—or are they sentenced to death as in some parts of the world? Is this why Oscar Wilde's books are banned there? Maybe CaZZ and Estelle were right. Maybe Mr. Oku and his partner left North Kristol to escape punishment, if not death. And if neither, maybe they moved to South Kristol because they weren't given the same rights as heterosexuals. Maybe there are no existing laws offering them the same benefits or protecting them from discrimination, bullying, and

193

other hate-related crimes. Can they get fired, refused service in restaurants, bullied in schools, or even brutally attacked or killed because of who they are? Maybe they're only allowed to exist, to operate like robots, deprived of the freedom to be and the right to love and be loved. What if North Kristol doesn't want me—and the world—to know anything about gays and lesbians there? What if they're controlling the information that enters South Kristol? What if . . .

My Codependency Poem

Forget the white chickens
and rain for now.

That red wheelbarrow, too.
So much brightness

in this room today
depends

solely
on a missed call

or a ZAP
with or without an emoji.

From: KenZ <antarctica#1@symphonic.com>
To: Ran <5xy2qd17@northkristol.federation.org>
Subject: out of the blue comes
Date: Sunday, 31 March

Hey Ran

I know you're extremely busy, so I'll try to be brief. I was doing laundry this afternoon when, out of the blue, a memory came speeding back to me. It was during one of our out-of-the-blue moments. You asked me why I sometimes went quiet on you, like a penny was not enough for my thoughts. I couldn't lie right off the bat, so I said the first truth that came to my mind. I confessed to you that I get like that whenever I feel a haiku is heading my direction. You laughed. Remember, Ran? I laughed along too, to cover my embarrassment. You thought I was joking, so you said, "Seriously, Ken Z?" I yupped my answer, said, "Haikus are a hard habit to break, Ran." Then you asked one of the most wonderful questions I have ever heard. "Ever go beyond seventeen syllables?" It was enough to make my heart jump. It sounded so new, so out of this world. It was marvelous and unforgettable, yet so simple. Only five ordinary words, but enough to build a small poem with them. "Ever go beyond seventeen syllables?" All I could do afterward was stutter, "N-n-not yet." Remember that, Ran? Remember my "Not yet" stuttering? I blushed with embarrassment. Two tiny words shaking out of my body the way this memory is stuttering loud and clear now. Not yet, not yet. Over and over . . .

Not yet,

Ken Z

PS Is this the end of our Antarctica, Ran?

Then I clicked SAVE DRAFT.

ESTELLE'S ENCORE ZAPS

SENT MONDAY 4/1, 12:58 P.M.

Where are you?
Playing hooky without me?
Useless—this haiku.

SENT MONDAY 4/1, 7:05 P.M.

Ill or chilling?

SENT MONDAY 4/1, 7:10 P.M.

You sick, or lovesick?
Play Air Supply's *Greatest Hits*.
I'm all out of love.

SENT MONDAY 4/1, 9:07 P.M.

Seriously, you okay?
What's wrong, Ken Z?
Zap me. Please.

SENT TUESDAY 4/2, 12:09 A.M.

Night, Sweet Prince.
Can't wait to see you tomorrow, I hope.
Miss you sorely.

TUESDAY, 2 APRIL

Dear Oscar: Can I
Consider this muddled day
Another false start?

The False-Start List

Superstar doomed dreams (kindergarten). Tap dance and voice
lessons. Instructor refunded my mom's money for the remaining
sessions and told her flat out that I was no Fred Astaire. "He's
got rhythm but not the Gershwin kind."

Entrepreneur (second grade). Selling Sunday papers at a major
intersection. The newspaper turned out to be ten times heavier
than me. I lasted for two Sundays.

Mad scientist (third grade). My mom couldn't afford my dream
microscope. So I got the next best thing—a magnifying glass,
which led me to the wonders of burning leaves and bugs. It
became a craze after I did a show-and-tell for some classmates
during lunch recess. Teacher found out about it, reported me to
my mom, and that pretty much sums up my life as a scientist.

Spelling bee (fifth grade). Made it all the way to the finals, then
bombed because of a Yiddish word that nobody, except for
Ivan Singer, knew. K-N-I-S-H. knish: noun; a fried or baked
dumpling stuffed with filling.

Rock climbing (sixth grade). Don't ask.

French (eighth grade), where I discovered I lacked a certain "Je ne
sais quoi. Pour quoi? Je ne sais pas."

The Vampire Trilogy, by Charlotte Madison (ninth, tenth, and eleventh grades). Reading about Mormon vampires struggling to keep their virginity can be interesting. But stretched out over three volumes is another thing entirely. I sleepwalked through the first book, Jupiter Rising.

Bunburying at Mirage (twelfth grade, spring break). Where's the fun in pretending to be rich if you have to budget?

Ran (seventeen days ago). (And counting.)

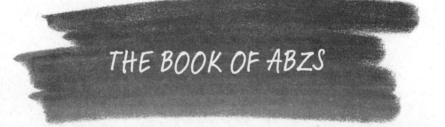

THE BOOK OF ABZS

LITTLE MIRACLES, PART II

Every minute
Lives a blue-throated hummingbird's
Thousand heartbreaks.

What's happening to me? One minute, I'm writing a list to stretch happiness a little longer.

The next, I'm writing a list to keep myself from drowning.

THE PRAYER

I pray it wasn't all
a one-man act
to spice up his day.
I pray he'll knock on my door
from out of my blue
with a large pizza
and a supersized grin.
It doesn't matter
if he wakes me up
from the most beautiful dream.
I'll be grateful
for the disruption
and won't badger him
with questions.
I pray he Zaps me now.
An emoji will do
or a semisad face
or harlequin tears
or a wave with a white-gloved hand.
How I wish
I didn't have to crave
such wishes,
for there are more important prayers
like world peace
and his safety
and me being kinder
to my friends
and myself.

Above all,
I pray for goodbyes
to not last this long
or matter
this much.

FORECAST FOR WEDNESDAY, 3 APRIL

Without Ran—mostly
April rain with Ken Zero
Visibility.

The Pyramid of Stupidity

Friday, 4 April

I did another stupid thing today. I went back to school after missing classes for three days. I was already getting used to staying home and even thought of only going back to school to take tests. I don't care if my grades plummet because of my absences. I don't care if I don't graduate with honors. I'll still graduate, unless I bomb on the finals. All it means is that I won't get to march and receive my diploma from the principal, while Mr. Oku places a cheap-looking golden cord around my neck to mean I'm Somebody in an auditorium full of people who don't really care. No, I don't need the extra attention.

The moment I entered the room, I saw CaZZ and Estelle. It was awkward. I didn't know whether or not to say hi, too afraid I'd end up making a fool of myself. I should've turned around and headed back home. That's what I should've done. It was torture, to be in the same room with the two people I consider my only friends since birth. A friendship that is now jeopardized. Thanks to me.

CaZZ snubbed me. Estelle, too, though I detected a faint smile. But that could've been wishful thinking. She's probably

211

211

fed up. I don't blame her. She Zapped me all weekend. The least I could've done was reply. I'm so stupid. I should make a "Stupid List" and put myself at the top.

By second period, I wanted to pick up my bag, go straight to the school clinic, fake a migraine. I've gotten so good at feigning illness that if not for my mom, who can read my body temperature just by looking at me, I would've stayed home until graduation. Maybe I should bunbury as a phony suffering from chronic headaches. But what I'm going through is worse than a migraine. I don't know how to describe it, except that it's a heavy, sinking feeling, like a ghost sitting on my chest. And it's getting worse. Every time it comes, my heart starts beating real fast and all I want to do is run home, lock myself in my room, and pray I disappear.

Soon as the dismissal bell rang, I bolted for the door. I looked behind and was relieved not to see CaZZ and Estelle trailing after me. But instead of going straight home, stupid me went to hide in the library, which is the most obvious place to find me. Sure enough, they showed up. CaZZ was the first to shatter the silence. "What's with the bad attitude?"

I pretended to be deaf. I stood up, tossing my notebook and pen into my backpack.

"Oh, so now you're giving us the hypermute treatment?" She was on a roll, and when CaZZ is on a roll, there's no stopping her.

Estelle broke in gently. "Dude, we miss you megamuch, you know."

I fought hard not to look at her. It was killing me, but I wasn't going to let her gentleness break me; no, not this time. When she realized that she wasn't going to get a word out of me, she changed her tactic. "What the hell is your problem, Ken Z? No Zaps. No missed or butt calls."

I kept quiet.

They wouldn't give up, until, finally, I told them nothing was the matter.

"Nada de nada," Estelle said. "Then why are you acting like—"

"An asshole," CaZZ blurted.

"We barely saw you last month," Estelle said. "We already forgave ourselves for forgiving you. Right, CaZZ?"

CaZZ didn't say anything. She was too upset for words.

"Urgh, Ken Z," Estelle continued.

CaZZ finally spoke. "He's punishing us, Estelle. That's what he's doing. Punishing us for whatever we did to him."

"You didn't do anything, okay?" I interjected.

CaZZ heard the sarcasm in my voice. "Don't snap at us."

"Yeah, dudeness," Estelle said.

"Whatever, dude," CaZZ said. "I'm getting tired of your charades, Ken Z. Tired of worrying about you. If you don't want to tell us what the hell is happening to you, then don't. Stay in the goddamn dark. You can rot there, for all I care."

I grabbed my bag and headed for the door.

Estelle tried to stop me.

"Let him go, Estelle," CaZZ said. "That's right, Ken Z, walk away. You seem to be doing a lot of that lately. But no matter how fast you go, you're not going anywhere. You live on an island, stupid. You'll only go in circles."

She was right. But I didn't care. All I wanted was to get away from them as fast and as far as possible. But no matter how fast I was, it wasn't enough. Because the sinking feeling returned to weigh me down. And with every step I took, it got heavier and heavier.

From Here to Hell

Saturday, 6 April

Today I did the ~~unthinkable~~ unforgivable. I went back to Mirage ~~hoping praying~~ looking for Ran. Two hours wasted at the bus stop. Not a very good sign. When I got there, I was nearly turned away because of my collarless shirt. ~~Luckily,~~ One of the mall security personnel recognized me. He probably saw me with Ran. That's me: Ken Z, memorable only by association. I went straight to Buddha's Joint. It was empty. I hung around there for an hour. ~~Just in case he~~ Then I looked everywhere for him, my eyes working triple time, making sure I did not miss a single face. I promised myself that if I bumped into him ~~please~~ just one ~~final~~ more time, I would not make a scene. He wouldn't have to utter a single word. I would've been okay with that. A simple hello ~~I'd be okay with that~~ would've been more than enough. I scoured the mall twice before I went back to Buddha's Joint. I stayed there for I don't know how long, two, three hours, my concentration seesawing between *The Trials of Oscar Wilde* and every customer that walked into the restaurant. What was I doing? Going crazy, that's what. Being stupid, that's what. It was around four p.m. when I finally ~~mustered~~ had the ~~strength~~ guts to leave. I didn't want to. I could've hung around Mirage for another day, month, year, ~~waiting,~~ building my tower of disappointments. Thank God I still had some brain cells left to tell me, "Get real, Ken Z. He's never going to show up. Stamp it on that thick skull of yours. You don't belong here, anyway. Go now before you miss the bus from hell! Go home and wallow in your pathetic journal and lists and haikus." I was ~~dejected~~ ~~upset~~ so angry at myself. How did I go from happiness to hell? Oscar once said, "If the gods wish to punish us, they will answer our prayers." If that is so, then why are they ignoring mine? Or are these the side effects of an answered prayer? Damaged days? Countless hours of banging my head against memories? They're ~~unbeatable matchless~~ useless now. I don't want them. They only remind me of ~~sorrow pain~~ my stupidity. Today's mad ride to hell is the last straw. I will not be tempted again. I don't care what Oscar says about temptation. He shouldn't ~~talk~~ be giving advice to anybody. Temptation—bah! Look where temptation got him. Look what temptation's given me. I'm so ~~stupid~~ pathetic. I'm just like Oscar, repeating my madness with the same guy. Except my story is worse. At least with Oscar, his Bosie stuck around until the very end. He remained the jerk that Oscar ~~had fallen in love obsessed over~~ went crazy over. But at least he didn't pull a Houdini on Oscar, unlike Ran. Ran, who is now a ~~memory~~ ghosty waiting for me to ~~erase void~~ forget him.

The I'm-So-Pathetic List

*Checking my phone four trillion times a day to see if he's
Zapped me.*

*Playing our "De-Lovely" song-and-dance number over and over in
my mind.*

Taking the number eight bus to Mirage to look for him.

*Thinking of applying for a travel visa to North Kristol, knowing
I'll be denied.*

Devoting an entire list to him.

Swinging back and forth between hope and hopelessness.

My heart jumping at the sight of every shaven-head guy.

Unable to read anything without seeing him between the lines.

Lying to close friends.

*Memorizing his last text, date and time included. Monday,
18 March. 2:23 a.m.*

Holding my breath until he resurfaces from ghosting.

The Mask of the Heart

We are never who we are. This is what Oscar Wilde's plays and stories have taught me. *The Picture of Dorian Gray*. *The Importance of Being Earnest*.

We are never who we are. Just a bunch of bunburyists inventing identities to get the most fun out of life. Perpetual adventurers who carry with them several shadows.

But how many "I's" do I need to start feeling good about myself again? How many masks must I wear to cover up the pain? And how do I get over this waiting and wanting for the heart to stop remembering?

GHOSTING: DAY 22

Should I surrender?
I'm running out of prayers
to save this madness.

Utterly

In the dream, I am in Oscar's suite at the Grand Hotel in Brighton, England. The year is 1893; the month, March. I am standing beside the window, watching the rain chase people off the street. Oscar is bedridden with the flu. He's been waiting for Bosie to return from his ghosting. Bosie left two days ago, slamming the door as Oscar pleaded with him not to leave. Oscar's condition has gotten worse since then. He wants to return to London, where his wife can nurse him, but he's so weak he can't even get up to fetch water or use the bathroom without my help.

"If not for your kindness, Ken Z," Oscar says, "my life would've ended in this drab room. I can only imagine the headlines. 'Celebrated playwright killed in a duel with wallpaper.'"

"Where's Bosie?" I ask.

"Out. Probably cruising for trouble."

"He should be here, taking care of you," I say. "You're only sick because you caught it from him."

Less than a week ago, Bosie was practically bedridden, coughing and delirious from high fever. Worried that Bosie wouldn't recover, Oscar set aside family obligations and the play he was working on to attend to him. And now that Oscar needs him, he's nowhere to be found, traipsing around London and dining in fancy restaurants with Oscar's money.

"I don't understand how he can be so cruel to you," I say.

"Bosie, unfortunately, inherited his father's mean temper," Oscar replies.

"Does he even like you, Oscar? Because he doesn't act like he does."

"I want to think so. I remember when we first met, we were inseparable."

Tears well in his eyes as he reminisces about their first months together.

"Nothing could come between us. We traveled everywhere, wined and dined in the most expensive restaurants. At my expense, of course. Bosie treated me as if I were his bank."

"And now?"

"Now a day does not pass without us getting into fights."

"How miserable!"

"We'd rather fight and ruin each other than be separated," Oscar says. "But this is nothing unusual."

"Nothing unusual? It's not normal, Oscar."

"We mean a lot to each other." Oscar pauses to cough. I rush to his bedside, rub his back. He points to the glass pitcher. It's empty.

Just then, Bosie storms in.

Oscar breathes a sigh of relief.

"Bosie, where have you been?" I ask.

He ignores me, walks straight up to Oscar. He tries to coax the sick playwright out of bed. He tells him friends are waiting for them in the lobby. "Get dressed, Oscar," he says. "Now!"

Oscar shakes his head, begs him to stop.

"He's sick!" I yell at Bosie. "He can barely stand!"

None of my words register. It's as if I'm a ghost in the room.

"Please, Bosie," Oscar says, gesturing for a glass of water.

Bosie glares at him. He doesn't budge. Eyes widening like a madman's, he laughs right in his face.

"Don't mock me, dear lad," Oscar pleads.

But delight and cruelty are one and the same to Bosie. He starts berating Oscar, accuses him of social climbing, of being a penny-pincher. "What a complete bore you are!" he shouts.

"Bosie, please do not make a scene with me," Oscar says. "It kills me and I cannot listen to you saying hideous things."

Bosie continues to taunt him. "You're repulsive!"

My hand balls into a fist, ready to attack Bosie should he lay a hand on Oscar.

"When you are not on your pedestal," Bosie says, "you are utterly uninteresting."

"Stop," Oscar begs. "You're breaking my heart, Bosie. I'd sooner be rented all day than have you be bitter, unjust, and horrid."

"What about you?" I tell Bosie. "You're nothing but a second-rate poet, an entitled bully cursed with your father's temper."

Bosie turns to me. "Speak for yourself!" he says. "You're just as pathetic as your hero. When are you two going to realize that you both have been played?"

Bosie walks toward me, snarling like a rabid dog. I take a step back.

In the background, I can hear Oscar begging him not to hurt me.

As he draws closer and closer, his face starts to morph into Ran's. Until there's no sign of Bosie left.

I back off until I hit a wall. Ran grins. He's taking delight in terrorizing me. He jabs his finger, hard, into my chest. He strokes my cheek with the same finger. He pushes his weight against me, whispering "You're pathetic" in my ear. Oscar begs him to stop. Finally, he leaves, slamming the door behind him.

In the mirror, I see Oscar's reflection. It is that of a sad and troubled man. "What have I done, Ken Z?" he cries out. "I shouldn't have left home. I shouldn't have strayed from my wife and sons. I have neglected my duties as husband and father."

"You shouldn't have fallen for him, Oscar," I say. "You shouldn't have listened to your heart."

I wake up, hearing myself repeating these words, again and again.

You shouldn't have fallen, Ken Z.

You shouldn't have listened to your heart.

SUNDAY, 7 APRIL

From dusk-draped window
Brightness leaves me
Light by light by light.

MONDAY MORNING

Scrubbing the kitchen
Sink with memories, absence
Makes the heart grow ~~fonder~~ mold.

Backfire

Monday, 8 April

Wasn't in the mood for school, so I cut class after second period. It was easy. All I had to do was walk out of campus looking sickly and holding a piece of paper in case the ogre passing as campus security asked for it. He didn't. It was the same pass from last week when I went to the clinic suffering from a fake headache. I stayed in bed for the rest of the day and read *The Trials of Oscar Wilde* for the book club this Friday. The book's pretty thick, but it moves fast, like watching a two-hour courtroom drama unravel before me. My blood boiled while reading it. I was angry—at Bosie, at Bosie's father, at the Victorian society that turned its back on its celebrated playwright. Most of all, I was angry at Oscar, so much so that I couldn't bring myself to talk to him about it. I was afraid I'd say something I'd end up regretting.

I only wished Oscar had listened to his friends when they'd advised him not to take Bosie's father to court. If he had, he would've avoided his own downfall. There would've been more masterpieces from him. But he was too stubborn. Too proud?

Too vain? Whatever the reasons, he let Bosie talk him into pursuing the libel suit. Maybe they both thought he'd win the case easily. After all, he was Oscar Wilde, and all Oscar Wilde had to do was put on his charming and witty self to humor and win over the jurors. He'd forgotten that Victorian high society wore another mask: one that was vindictive, repressed, obsessed with morality, and against anything that deviated from the norm, especially sex between men.

Oscar's lawsuit backfired on him. At the trial, incriminating evidence was presented. Victorious, Bosie's father urged the Crown to prosecute Oscar. They did. It ended in a hung jury, so they tried him again and would've kept on until they reached a verdict of guilty. They were that bloodthirsty—those nineteenth-century vampires in top hats and coattails. Hate does that, brings out the evil and violent side of a person, a government, a society, a nation, to punish their own heroes.

I did not read beyond the second trial. I already knew what was going to happen. It would only make me more furious, force me to change my opinion of my hero, bring out unwanted feelings, thoughts, words.

MONDAY AFTERNOON

Scrubbing the kitchen
Sink with memories, absence
Makes the heart grow ~~mold~~ furious.

The Prison of Hope

TUESDAY, 9 APRIL. MIDDAY. MY BEDROOM.

OSCAR: And what are you reading now, dear boy?

ME: *De Profundis.*

OSCAR: Dear Lord.

ME: I know. You should've called it *De-Pressing.*

OSCAR: Why are you punishing yourself with my gloom? I've written many others—and they're more uplifting than that sad chapter in my life.

ME: I want to know what happened to you after the trial, Oscar. What prison life was like in England in those days. What you did to block out the pain. I don't want to read about it on the Internet. Half the things on there are fake anyway. I want it to come straight from you—your own words.

OSCAR: My *Inferno.* As narrated by me.

ME: Yes.

OSCAR: Let's see. . . . Well, in prison, there is only one season, Ken Z, and that is the season of sorrow. The very sun and moon seem taken from us. Outside, the day may be blue and gold, but the light that creeps down through the thickly muf-

fled glass of the small iron-barred window is gray and meager. I spent most of the day in solitary confinement. My world in those two years, Ken Z, measured thirteen feet long and seven feet wide and nine feet high. My bed was a piece of plank. Beside it was a chamber pot. I became an insomniac as a result.

ME: What did you do to pass the time?

OSCAR: I tidied up my room. Every day, the warden inspected my cell. Everything in it had to be clean and organized.

ME: Otherwise?

OSCAR: Punishment. The food was horrible. It turned my stomach, often resulting in violent diarrhea. Every day, after breakfast, which consisted of cocoa and brown bread, I and other prisoners were brought out to the prison yard to reunite with the sun. We were not allowed to converse. For an hour, we walked in circles, in absolute silence.

ME: How cruel.

OSCAR: And that was only the beginning of the day. In my first three months in prison, I was ordered to step on the treadwheel. Like a laboratory mouse, I climbed that staircase from hell for six hours nonstop. Another form of physical and mental torture was picking oakums. My fingertips bled and grew dull with pain. It was a tedious, mind-numbing task with no goal other than to punish the prisoner and drive him closer to madness. Every day, until I left the prison, I picked those ropes apart for ten hours.

ME: Did anyone visit you?

OSCAR: At first, no. When I was finally permitted to receive visitors, I could only have one every three months, and only for twenty minutes.

ME: Jesus. Did they at least give you books to read, or pen and paper?

OSCAR FALLS SILENT. TEARS ARE WELLING IN HIS EYES. SHAKING HIS HEAD, HE CONTINUES WITH HIS STORY.

OSCAR: They knew I was a writer, Ken Z. They knew the tools I could not live without were books, paper, and pen. So essential are they to the literary man, so vital are they for the preservation of mental balance. With these tools, I could combat the silence they had condemned me to. By denying me pen and paper, they'd perfected my miserable state. By denying me books, they'd cut me off from all knowledge of the external world and the movements of life. I was allowed only two books to read from the prison "library," which contained hardly a score of books suitable for an educated man. I was deprived of everything that could've soothed, distracted, and healed my wounded and shaken mind. It wasn't until there was a change of chairman on the prison commission that I, after nearly eighteen months, was finally granted writing materials and books more suitable for brainpower.

ME: They really wanted you to suffer.

OSCAR: The prison system under Queen Victoria was not meant to reform convicts, Ken Z, but to punish them, again and again, until they were stripped of everything—dignity, hope, the determination to rebuild their lives upon their release.

ME: Who visited you?

OSCAR: The two most important people in my life—my wife and my dear friend Robbie. It was my wife who broke the news to me that my mother had died.

I START TO TEAR UP. I DIDN'T REALIZE HE'D GONE THROUGH
SUCH HELL DURING THOSE TWO YEARS IN PRISON. BUT IT
WASN'T JUST HARD LABOR THEY SENTENCED HIM WITH. THEY
ALSO DULLED HIS SENSES, DEGRADED HIM, PRACTICALLY DROVE
HIM TOWARD THE IRREVERSIBLE PATH TO MADNESS.

ME: I would've killed myself, Oscar.

OSCAR: They wanted me to.

ME: But you survived the ordeal.

OSCAR: And I owe it all to Major Nelson, who granted me pen,
paper, and books. Oh, Ken Z, I felt alive. Because I was writing again, and reading books. Writing and reading—without
those two I don't think I would've survived my time in hell.
Remember that, dear heart, especially during your darkest
hours when nothing seems to bear a semblance of light.

DE PROFUNDIS

*A Manual for
Idiots, by the author
of Downsized Haikus.*

THE MASK OF SORROW

Behind this sorrow
Resides another sorrow
And then another. . . .

The Hour of Sadness

Wednesday, 10 April. It is almost two p.m.

This is Oscar's haunted hour. Two p.m. The exact time of his disgrace. The date was 13 November 1895. The place—Clapham Junction station. Oscar is being transferred to another prison. Dressed in a convict's jumpsuit, he stands shakily on the platform. He wishes the ground beneath him to open up so it can swallow him. He doesn't care if it's a gutter with—or without—stars. At this point, the deeper hell is, the better. Anything is better than the glare of commuters.

They all stop to steal glances at him. They are wondering who he could be. They point to the handcuffs that he tries to hide beneath his sleeves. He starts to waver. He's afraid he's going to faint again, like he did in the prison chapel. He hit the side of his head on the floor and practically busted his eardrum. It got infected, and he ended up in the infirmary for two months. He shuts his eyes, takes deep breaths to steady his nerves.

. . .

He prays for the November rain to fall harder on the roof, to drown out the voices mocking him. He raises his head momentarily to the station clock. It is quarter past two. The train to Reading Gaol, where he's being transferred to, will not be arriving for another fifteen minutes. To shut off the slow ticking of the clock in his head, he busies himself with a mental list—an inventory of his possessions that had been auctioned off to pay his debts and his lawyers' fees. These included his books, manuscripts, copyrights to his plays and published articles; his art collection, writing desks, four-poster beds, picture frames, down to the door scraper and the carpet that covered the staircase. Everything he'd ever owned had been sold to the highest bidder.

A broken smile flashes briefly across his sullen face. His two sons, Cyril and Vyvyan, enter his thoughts. For a moment, he finds refuge in remembering them and almost forgets the eyes hounding him. Just then, someone on the platform recognizes him. Word spreads fast, like a killer virus. The crowd thickens, buzzes like flies around a wounded animal. They jostle each other to get a good look at him. They sneer at him, douse him with names; their spit, like gasoline, waiting to be ignited.

He was once the wit of the West End with two sold-out plays running simultaneously. Now he is showered with insults and curses, with hatred so pure and perfect.

Six months ago, he was the toast of London high society.
He was invincible.
Or so he thought.

. . .

Oscar shuts his eyes tight, his teeth biting hard into his lower lip. He tastes blood. Like rust. The jeers continue to swell inside his head. He will die alone and—unlike the heroes in his fairy tales—unloved. He will never be able to reclaim his glorious past. He will never see his two sons again. He has thrown his life away, tossed whatever happiness and meaning it had.

His life—reduced to a confetti of ashes.

Weeks later, inside his cell, he will sit down to revisit the horror of that November afternoon in *De Profundis* and write: *After that was done to me, I wept every day at the same hour and for the same space of time.*

This incident took place over a century ago. And yet I can hear it reverberate loud and clear in my head, as if it's happening now. I think of CaZZ and Estelle and myself and the others who have been—and continue to be—bullied, because we dare to be ourselves. Because we look different or worship a different god or speak the same language but with an accent. I think of those who, to stop the hurting, give up on life, place a noose around their sorrows, and hang like bruised fruit on trees, or leap off buildings or bridges. Anything to end the hurting.

. . .

I think of hatred so powerful it ties you to a fence or hooks you up to a life support machine. It is almost three p.m. The mocking laughter continues exploding in my head. The bloodthirsty mob has invaded my room and formed a ring around me like a circle of sharks. I am at the heart of their loathing. They scoff at me, spit names at me. They take turns pushing and punching me. They hold me down, duct-tape my mouth, my eyes. They want to silence my every word. They want to extinguish what light is left in me. They want to choke my language, slice my every vein of determination to keep on fighting, rebelling, and resisting just to be me.

The It's-Not-Hard-to-Imagine List

It's not hard to imagine getting bullied for being you.
Be yourself and minds will narrow.
Speak your mind and death threats will follow.
This is how The Book of Hate begins.
It's not hard to imagine CaZZ as Bullied Holiday in
　　Tranny Sings the Blues.
It's not hard to imagine another CaZZ gasping for
　　tomorrow.
Waking up neither safe nor sound.
Not feeling dynamite enough to blow up the hurt.
It's not hard to imagine some of the teachers at our
　　school saying CaZZ deserved it because she was too
　　comfortable in her own skin.
It's not hard to imagine another Estelle picked on because
　　she's uncategorizable, a queerious
　　who makes up her own words and does not care if the
　　world understands her or not.
It's not hard to imagine another Ken Z getting teased for
　　being too geeky, too much into books,
　　too into Oscar Wilde to be a macho man: skinny legs,
　　skinnier arms.

*It's not hard to imagine outsiders of the world uniting, not
giving in or giving up or turning the other cheek.
It's not hard to imagine finding strength in the darkest
spaces, during the saddest hours.*

WEDNESDAY-NIGHT INERTIA

From insomnia
To this troubled haiku:
Let me count the ways.

Alternative Torture

Thursday, 11 April

Woke up past ten this morning. My mother didn't wake me up. She probably thinks I'm still sick—or not ready to face my friends. I was up all night reading *De Profundis*. Sad as it was, I forced myself to read it to the very end, hoping that when I finished it my own suffering, too, would be gone. But it only made me more depressed and angry and sad and hopeless, as if my situation were not tortuous enough.

I got an email from Mr. Oku, asking me if I was all right. He was concerned because of my absences, and said that if I continue to miss any more of his classes, excused or not, he has no recourse but to drop my grade to a B. He closed his letter by wishing me well and hoped to see me in class tomorrow, which is also when our book club meets.

Then I searched the Web for the one topic that I shouldn't have, fearing I would never get up and leave my room. Sure enough, there were thirty-nine million results for "Oscar Wilde." I narrowed it down to "Oscar Wilde book clubs around the world." Better. Only 1.5 million results. I stopped at the top

of the third page, my eyes hooked by the catchy title, "So you think you know Oscar Wilde?" It was from a Romanian blogger. In this entry, he compiled a list of facts and tidbits about our favorite writer:

"Did you know Oscar Wilde had a younger sister named Isola who died when she was only ten years old and Oscar was twelve?"

"Did you know that he was so affected by her death that when he died in a dingy hotel room in Paris, they found an envelope containing a lock of Isola's hair under his pillow?"

"Did you know that Oscar's first 'boyfriend' was not Bosie but a Canadian named Robbie Ross? Oscar was already married and the father of two when he had his first gay experience."

Then, an entry about Oscar that I did not want to believe. But there it was, highlighted in dark pink:

"Did you know that Oscar and Bosie remained lovers, even after Oscar was released from prison and sought exile in Paris and Naples?"

I wanted to throw my laptop across the room. After everything that Bosie put him through, he took him back? No! Please, Oscar, tell me this isn't true. Tell me this is only an alternative fact, something that could've happened but didn't, a work of a fan fictionist who was into self-torture.

Betrayal for Beginners

THURSDAY, 11 APRIL. AFTERNOON. MY BEDROOM.

OSCAR: What's the matter, Ken Z? You seem upset.

ME: Oh, my God, please tell me it's fake news!

OSCAR: I have no idea what you're talking about, dear boy.

ME: You and Bosie. Did you take him back after you left prison?

OSCAR BOWS HIS HEAD IN SHAME.

ME: Oh, my God! So it's true. Why, Oscar? After all the things he did to you?

OSCAR: Bosie ruled my heart, Ken Z.

ME: He ruined it. He ruined your family, too. You had everything—fame, fortune, friends—but you let this punk control you. Why?

OSCAR: I don't know, Ken Z. All I know is that I loved him.

ME: You call that love? That's obsession. You were so obsessed with Bosie that you traded a life of security, glory, and peace of mind for madness and instability.

OSCAR: Why destruction has such a fascination for me—I will

never know. Love never fails, my dear boy. When one is in love, one begins by deceiving oneself and ends by deceiving others. That is what the world calls romance.

ME: Romance? Listen to yourself, Oscar. That's the voice of Insanity talking!

OSCAR: Perhaps.

ME: Perhaps? It is! After everything that's happened, you still took him back?

OSCAR: It was psychologically inevitable, Ken Z.

ME: He didn't torture you enough? It was because of him that you ended up in prison. Have you forgotten?

OSCAR: I had nothing, Ken Z.

ME: Nothing?

OSCAR: Yes, nothing. When the gates of Reading Gaol finally let me out, I had nothing. No money. No family. My wife was gone; the law had already taken away my children. Had my wife allowed me to see my boys, my life would've been different.

ME: Don't blame your wife, Oscar. You did it to yourself!

OSCAR: I never ventured to blame Constance for her action. I take full responsibility. I regret what I did to my wife. I regret that I was not able to see her before she died and beg for her forgiveness.

ME: She was ready to take you back, Oscar, on the condition that you cut off your ties with Bosie. You promised her you'd never see him again, that you'd kill him if you ever ran into him. You wrote this in your letter to her. I *read* this in *De Profundis*. Yet . . .

OSCAR: Please, Ken Z, don't torture my ghosts. They're already at peace.

ME: Peace?

OSCAR: Please, Ken Z, try to understand my disposition. My wife died just months after I was released from prison. So, as you can see, I had no one. But Bosie offered me love. In my loneliness and disgrace, he offered me love, Ken Z . . . and I . . . I turned naturally to him.

ME: You had your friends.

OSCAR: Ken Z, have compassion for this wretched stupid man whose only mistake was to love without the intent to hurt anyone, especially his wife and his sons.

ME: But you did.

OSCAR: Please, Ken Z.

ME: They, too, were tainted with shame—*yours*. They had to change their names to protect themselves from your disgrace.

OSCAR: My dear boy, your words are bullets piercing my heart tonight.

ME: How many times did Bosie have to torture you before you realized he didn't love you?

OSCAR: Bosie did love me, Ken Z.

ME: He did not. He only sought you when he needed your wallet. You were his bank, not his beloved.

OSCAR: Why are you condemning me? Bosie filled me with desire. And horror. And madness. And passion. He tempted me with a life I could never have imagined. He offered me the rare privilege of courting another kind of beauty, a different type of danger.

ME: Talking to you is useless. How could I have ever looked up to you?

OSCAR: My dear boy, I never asked you to put me on a pedestal. I understand your rage, Ken Z. Believe me, I do. You're angry right now. You're filled with hate.

ME: Understatement of the night.

OSCAR: But I beg of you, dear Ken Z: don't let hate consume you as it did Bosie.

ME: Speak for yourself, Oscar. You let someone consumed by hatred rule your heart.

OSCAR: Bosie's my tragedy, Ken Z.

ME: You're mad.

OSCAR: My dear lad, no one wants their first kiss to blossom into an open wound. But because of what's happened to you, between you and Ran . . . you're now filled with remorse. . . .

ME: Remorse?

OSCAR: For letting Ran wake up your sleeping heart.

ME: Thanks to you.

OSCAR: *Moi?*

ME: You told me not to resist temptation. "Feast with the panther," as you said.

OSCAR: Because you sought my advice. My dear Ken Z, try to find expression for your sorrow. Turn your sadness into words.

ME: I'm so stupid. I should've known better than to listen to you.

OSCAR: Whenever a man does a thoroughly stupid thing, it is always from the noblest of motives.

ME: All this is a big mistake.

OSCAR: Call it experience, Ken Z. Everyone else does. I'm sorry such a grand adventure has misled you to the path of disappointment.

ME: Disappointment? Try "tragedy."

OSCAR: There are two tragedies. One is not getting what one wants, and the other is getting it.

ME: Well, I must be lucky. I got both.

OSCAR: I'm sorry.

ME: Please, Oscar. Go away. Leave me alone.

OSCAR: Ken Z.

ME: Now!

OSCAR: As you wish, dear heart, as you wish.

AFTER A GREAT PAIN . . .

I don't want the chill
I don't want the stupor
you can keep the letting go
so come and take it
there is no room for it
in this room tonight
this is not a poem
this is nothing
preparing for more
nothing.

From: KenZ <antarctica#1@symphonic.com>
To: Ran <5xy2qd17@northkristol.federation.org>
Subject: Dear Ran
Date: Thursday, 11 April

Or whoever whatever wherever you are. It was there all along, wasn't it? In *De Profundis,* the book you gave me when we first met. That was the clue, right? A book about a man who falls for another man so badly that his obsession destroys him. I should've paid more attention. I shouldn't have allowed myself to fall so easily. So what if you were also wild about Oscar? Who cares about the mystery of serendipity and meant-to-bes? How stupid of me to believe in fate and destiny.

Don't worry. I'm not blaming you. I blame myself. Entirely, utterly. You were only doing your job, Ran. Ran. Is that even your real name? Or are you only Ran when you're in South Kristol bunburying as Dorian Gray's twin who surfaced from the underworld to deliver me my sentence? And when you handed the book to me, it came with a kiss.

You stuck around to make sure I obeyed the script. Why else would someone like you, debonair and privileged, exert so much time and effort to be with someone like me? So when you gave me the book and said, "Here, have it," you were really saying: "Take it, Ken Z, and read it. It's an old story that never gets tired. Oscar Wilde wrote it exclusively for us, about us. Read it carefully so you know what I'm about to do to you."

Today marks ~~twenty-four~~ ~~twenty-twenty~~ twenty-six days of ~~our~~ ~~your~~ absence.

Ken Z

Then I pressed hard on the backspace key
until it erased every single letter of every single word
that spelled out every sound of memory.

LAST WISH

If there is one thing I want most
right now, it is to return everything good
and beautiful back to the gods.

Return the happiness and those hours wasted
on laughing and longing.

Return the sudden bursts of joy
that shattered those awkward moments.

Return, too, the hummingbird's heartbeats
with its light nest of surprises,
and the memory of the moon,
bright as tonight,
lighting up this sleepless hour.

In Carcere et Vinculis

"On the same day that Oscar was charged with immoral conduct, over five hundred men fled England," Mr. Oku says. "What began as a libel lawsuit ended up being one of the most controversial trials in Britain's history."

"Where did they go?" Tanya asks.

"They went to the Continent," Mr. Oku replies. "Most of them to Paris, where homosexuality was more tolerated."

"They were afraid they were going to be arrested next, that's why," Matt remarks.

"It was a witch hunt," CaZZ says, "and they were using Oscar Wilde as their poster boy."

"And 'witch hunt' best describes the atmosphere," Mr. Oku says.

"That's why they tried him again, remember?" CaZZ says.

"But can they do that?" Tanya asks. "Can they try him even if the trial ended in a hung jury?"

"They were out to crucify Oscar," CaZZ remarks.

"And use him as a warning to all the homosexuals in England," Estelle says.

"'The world mocks it and sometimes puts one in the pillory for it,'" Matt says, quoting one of Oscar Wilde's immortal lines uttered during the trials.

"Perfectly put," Mr. Oku says.

"And the prosecutors, egged on by the public, didn't stop until they sent Oscar to prison," CaZZ says.

"What a bunch of homophobes!" Tanya says.

"That's Queen Victoria's England for you," Estelle says.

"What about the lesbians?" Tanya asks. "Did they get arrested too?"

"They didn't exist back then," CaZZ says.

"Seriously?" Tanya asks.

"CaZZ is right," Mr. Oku says. "People in Victorian England didn't have the labels that we have today."

"You mean there weren't queers and queens and dykes and fags?" Tanya asks.

Mr. Oku smiles. "I'm sure they were around, Tanya," he says. "But these categories—'homosexuals,' 'gays,' 'lesbians,' 'queers'—did not emerge until the twentieth century."

"Ever heard the joke about the alternative version of Eden?" CaZZ asks.

Tanya shakes her head.

"Paradise began with Adam and Steve," CaZZ replies.

"And in the lesbian version, it began with Madam and Eve," Estelle says.

"That's a good one, Estelle," Matt says, laughing.

"During Oscar's time, one was arrested for immoral conduct, not because of sexual orientation," Mr. Oku says.

"So hate the sin but not the sinner?" Tanya asks.

"Unless you're gay," CaZZ blurts.

"Of course," Estelle seconds.

Mr. Oku seems to agree with them, because he's nodding. "And with the Criminal Law Amendment Act of 1885, it made it easier to convict anyone of gross indecency."

"What exactly does that mean?" Tanya says. "It sounds kind of gross!"

"Ask Ken Z." CaZZ's mention of my name makes me look up.

Tanya turns to me, but Matt ends up spelling it out for her. "Sex between men."

"What's so gross about that?" Tanya asks.

"Well, during Oscar's time, it was," Matt says, "and you went to prison for it."

"Victorians were fixated on immorality," Mr. Oku says.

"Welcome to Victoria's Secrets," Estelle says.

"Sounds like Church of New Hope," CaZZ says, referring to Matt's church.

"You know, I never understood why it's called that," Tanya says. "What happened to the old hope, Matt?"

"It died," I reply.

Everyone turns to me.

"Ken Z," Mr. Oku says. "I didn't expect that remark to come from you."

I apologize to Matt.

"No problem, Ken Z," Matt says.

"Where were we?" Mr. Oku says.

I look at my notes. "The Criminal Act of 1885."

"Thank you," he says. "That law made it easier to convict anyone of gross indecency because hard evidence was no longer required. You could send someone to prison so long as you had a reliable witness or two. That's how they were able to convict Oscar. *The Picture of Dorian Gray* was even used as evidence."

"But it's a work of fiction," Tanya argues.

"It's got immorality written all over it," Matt says. "It's got drugs, suicide, violence, murder—"

"Underground gays," Estelle cuts in.

"But it's fiction," Tanya insists.

"Not to those prudes and hypocrites," CaZZ says. "In their eyes, if Oscar Wilde could imagine these vices, then he was also capable of committing them."

"What I don't get is why Oscar didn't just move to Paris," Tanya says. "Why didn't he just get on the boat, along with those five hundred men? I'm sure they could've hidden him."

"It was already too late," Matt says.

"Actually, Matt, it wasn't," Mr. Oku says. "He still had time."

"So why didn't he?" Tanya asks.

"He didn't go because of his mother," I blurt out.

"Really?" Tanya says, incredulously.

Mr. Oku nods. "His mother told him that if he fled, he would stop being her son."

"So she'd rather send her own son to prison?" Tanya says. "That's messed up."

"It wasn't that simple," Mr. Oku says. "You have to take into consideration that Oscar was Irish. And given the long history of fighting between Ireland and England, it would've been a sign of cowardice if Oscar, an Irishman, fled."

Tanya is shaking her head.

Matt raises his hand.

"Yes, Matt," Mr. Oku says.

"What I don't get is why someone like Oscar would even waste his time on an asshole like Bosie," Matt says. "I mean, he was so brilliant."

"Apparently not," I quip.

"What do you mean?" Tanya says.

"He was self-destructive," I reply.

CaZZ darts me a look. I'm about to retreat back to my silent world when Mr. Oku asks me to expound.

"From what I've read, Oscar didn't have to sue Bosie's father," I say.

"Maybe Oscar had no choice," Tanya breaks in. "You guys ever thought of that?" She sounds very smug, as if she's the only one capable of producing such a thought. "I mean, wasn't Bosie's father a certified nutcase? Didn't he try several times to publicly humiliate Oscar? Maybe by Oscar taking him to court, it would put an end to the harassment. And bullying."

"That's what Oscar and Bosie had hoped," Matt says.

"But it didn't," I argue.

"Maybe he was better off just turning the other cheek," Matt says.

"I don't think Oscar had a choice," Estelle says. "Sooner or later, they would've gone after him. There was a witch hunt, remember?"

"Good point, Estelle," Mr. Oku says.

The room is clearly divided: those who think Oscar shouldn't have sued Bosie's father (Matt and me) versus those who argue that Oscar did the right thing (CaZZ and Estelle). Tanya is undecided.

"Oscar had too much pride," Matt remarks. "I mean, I love Oscar. He's brilliant and all, and I love his stories and plays, but he was too egotistic, too arrogant."

"That's the problem," I say. "Oscar couldn't accept the fact that someone had dared to humiliate him in public."

"But wouldn't you do the same, Ken Z?" Tanya asks. "If you were in Oscar's shoes, wouldn't you fight back?"

"Probably not," CaZZ remarks.

"Well, I know I would," Tanya says.

"Oscar didn't tolerate bullies, especially bullies like Bosie's father," CaZZ says, her voice rising.

"Bosie bullied Oscar, too," I say. "And Oscar let him treat him like shit."

"Oscar was such a masochist!" Tanya remarks. "Just like the birds in his fairy tales."

"Bosie and Oscar didn't have a healthy relationship," I continue. "They were constantly fighting."

"Oscar was only looking out for Bosie," CaZZ retorts. "He was afraid that if he cut his ties with Bosie, no one else would protect him from his monstrous father."

"But Bosie was a monster himself," I say.

"Why didn't Oscar just end it?" Tanya asks.

"Because he was weak," I say. "He kept forgiving Bosie and taking him back."

"Because Oscar was very forgiving," CaZZ argues. "He was that kind of a person, Ken Z. He never wished any ill feelings on anyone, including Bosie, who had hurt him so much."

"Oscar was obsessed," I say.

"He was in love," CaZZ retorts.

"Yes, he sure was," I say, sarcastically.

"And what do you know about love, Ken Z?" CaZZ says.

"Probably more than you," I want to tell her instead of: "He was in love with fatality, with self-destruction—"

"You're too into yourself to know what love is," CaZZ cuts in, drowning my words. "You're too cooped up in your sad-ass world of lists and haikus."

"CaZZ!" Estelle and Mr. Oku shout at the same time.

259

CaZZ backs off.

"I can totally relate to Oscar," Tanya cuts in, "because that's exactly how I get when I'm obsessed. Can't sleep. Can't eat. My world is only alive because of him. Every day is like Nightmare on Tanya Street, except I don't see it as a nightmare because I'm too into the guy, or even if I do and know it's not a good thing, I don't do anything about it because I can't because I'm hopeless, helpless, a pathetic piece of shit. So, unless you've been obsessed with someone, Ken Z, you wouldn't know what it's like to be in Oscar's shoes."

"Amen, Tanya!" CaZZ says.

Tanya's words sting. I don't think she intentionally meant to hurt me. But she's just summed up my life from spring break to the present.

I want to scream for help.

I want to reboot my life.

I want this pathetic part of ME to die.

But instead of shutting up, I blurt out, "Oscar deserved what he got. He saw it coming and he let it happen."

"God, Ken Z!" Estelle exclaims.

"My, Ken Z, aren't you full of words today," CaZZ says.

Estelle motions at me to shut up.

"Don't, Estelle," CaZZ says. "He's finally letting his true self come out!"

"CaZZ!" Mr. Oku says.

But CaZZ is relentless. "He's been wearing a mask all this time and he's finally tired of pretending."

"That's enough, CaZZ!" Mr. Oku says.

"CaZZ," Estelle says, trying to appease her. Then, with pleading eyes, she turns to me. "Ken Z, what's happening to you? You're acting like you hate Oscar."

"Hate?" I say.

"Yes. Hate. You have so much hate in you. And bitterness. And anger."

Tanya jumps in and corners me with: "Yeah, Ken Z. Where's all this hate coming from? I thought you loved Oscar."

I feel like I'm being ganged up on. "I'm not the one on trial here," I say.

"Who says you are?" Estelle says. "We're just asking a question."

"It's not hate," I say, as calmly as possible. "All I'm saying is that Oscar was as much to blame for his downfall as Bosie."

"And he did blame himself," Estelle says.

"Entirely," CaZZ adds.

"When the tables were turned, and Oscar had to defend himself from a government that wanted to punish him, only then did he realize that his trials were much bigger," Mr. Oku says.

"Bigger?" Tanya asks.

"That it wasn't just a trial about Oscar's pride, or Bosie's vengeance toward his father. In the end, it was a trial about love."

"Love?" I ask.

"Yes, Ken Z, love," Mr. Oku replies.

"Love that dares not speak its name," Matt interjects.

Mr. Oku nods. "Love that's rejected by the law. Love that's constantly getting pushed and shoved around, spat at, bullied to unconsciousness. Love that's viewed as polluted and filthy. Love that gets sentenced to prison with hard labor. Because it must be punished. It serves no purpose. It has no meaning. Oscar Wilde's trial—" He stops to clear his throat, then continues. "Oscar Wilde's trial is a trial about love in the time of hate."

The room falls silent. CaZZ and Tanya have lowered their heads, tears pelting their desks, while Estelle looks straight

ahead at the chalkboard, her eyes also glazed with tears. Even Matt's not afraid to show the world his feelings for Oscar: his eyes are wet too.

Everyone mourning for the man who defended such love.

Except me.

Coldhearted me.

Time to exit stage right.

And head back to the comfort of my own prison.

Shim Sham

Friday, 12 April. Late afternoon.

They're pissed. Royally.

They've been pounding on my door for the past ten minutes and have already started a heated argument with my next-door neighbor, a cranky old man whose disdain for the human species has reached an all-time high.

From my room, I can hear him telling them, "It's obvious he's not home!"

"Oh, he's home," CaZZ says, "he's just playing deaf."

"Take the hint and scram," my neighbor says.

They ignore him; their pounding becoming louder and louder.

"I'm calling the cops!" shouts the fat lady from the floor above mine who lives with ten thousand cats.

"Be our guest!" CaZZ yells. "Better call them now so they can get here by tomorrow."

"Ken Z," my next-door neighbor shouts, "if you don't open the freakin' door right now, I'm going to break it open myself, then break you in half!"

I get up and open the door, ready to punch my neighbor's lights out. Beside him, CaZZ and Estelle seethe with rage.

The old man turns to them. "There he is," he says. "Now you can kill him." Exit the misanthrope.

I don't say anything. I can't even look at them.

"What the hell's wrong with you?" CaZZ says, storming into the living room. She's fuming, ready to punch me in the face. Estelle closes the door behind her.

"Nothing's wrong," I finally say. Wrong answer. It only aggravates them more.

"Estelle, give him a mask so he can lie better," CaZZ says.

Estelle shakes her head at me. It's her turn to explode. "You've been MIA in our lives for weeks," she says. "I wouldn't call that nothing. And when we do see you, you're barely present. Then, this afternoon"—she's so upset she can barely get the words out—"you went off on Oscar, saying he deserved all that shit that happened to him. Like, what the fuck was that all about, Ken Z?"

I want to say that he did deserve it. But I know better than to fan their fire.

"Ken Z, you're drifting from us," Estelle says. "Why?"

"Did we do anything to push you away?" CaZZ asks. The gentleness in her tone catches me off guard. It makes me look at the two of them. Big mistake. They look as lost and helpless and angry as I have been these past few weeks.

"Talk to us, Ken Z," Estelle pleads.

I avert my gaze. The heavy sinking feeling is back. I can feel my legs trembling, my heart beating in my throat. I open my mouth, but the words won't come out, lodged in the center of my chest. Then, suddenly, I hear myself say, "I met someone."

CaZZ and Estelle exchange looks. Their suspicions are finally confirmed.

"When?" CaZZ asks.

"During spring break?" Estelle guesses.

I nod. "I'm so stupid," I say. "I actually fell for it."

"Dude," Estelle says.

"I actually believed it was real," I continue. "Stupid love. Stupid me."

"Don't beat yourself up over it, Ken Z," CaZZ says. "We're all suckers for it."

"Yeah, Ken Z," Estelle says.

"Everyone falls, Ken Z," CaZZ says. "Everyone hurts. That's the sucky part about love."

"I really fell for it," I say. "It was so real, that he was sincere—"

"He?" CaZZ cuts in. Estelle hushes her.

I stop. I want to take back my disclosure but it's too late. No backing out now. That's the minus about confessing. Once you open up, all the locked-up words come rushing out like a stampede of wild horses.

"I didn't know myself," I say. "I swear to you guys, I didn't know. Everything happened so fast that I . . ."

"It's okay, Ken Z," Estelle says.

"Was I in denial all this time?" I ask.

Estelle shakes her head. "No, you weren't. Besides, who cares? It's just a label and you don't need it unless you're certain of what you really want and who you truly are. Right, CaZZ?"

"Hundred percent," CaZZ replies.

A moment of silence before the barrage of questions.

"Do we know him?" Estelle asks.

"No," I reply.

"Where'd you meet him?" CaZZ jumps in.

"Mirage," I say.

Estelle and CaZZ look at each other and simultaneously exclaim, "Mirage?"

"Yes," I say.

They exchange *hmmm* glances. I can read the smiles on their faces.

"More," Estelle says. "We want more."

"Yeah, Ken Z," CaZZ cuts in. "What's his name?"

"Ran."

"Ran?"

"As in 'ransom'?" Estelle asks.

"More like 'ran away,'" I say.

CaZZ stifles a laugh. "How old?"

"Seventeen."

"Face pic?"

I shake my head, wishing I had taken one.

"What does he look like?" CaZZ asks.

"You're going to think I'm crazy, but he kind of reminded me of Dorian Gray. Not just his looks, but his mannerisms, the way he talked," I say, remembering how Ran had this intense look on his face when he was talking or listening to me, like every word I said mattered.

"Are you serious?" CaZZ asks.

"Ken Z wouldn't lie about something like that," Estelle says.

I begin describing him to them. "He had blond hair, but I think it was dyed."

"Dyed?" CaZZ asks.

"The roots were showing; it was more like brown."

CaZZ and Estelle exchange more *hmmm* glances.

"What about his eyes?"

"Gray," I reply, "like your brothers'."

"So he's mixed," Estelle remarks.

"Like practically everyone on this island," CaZZ says. "Mixed. And messed up."

"Our Ken Z fell in love with a guy who could pass for Dorian Gray," Estelle says.

"A mongrel version of Dorian Gray," CaZZ corrects her.

"Dorian Gray and Ken Z, the Dork," I say.

"Dude, you're cute with a capital Q," Estelle says.

"If only he believed it," CaZZ tells Estelle.

I refuse the compliment.

CaZZ throws it back to me. "Ken Z, he wouldn't have approached you if you weren't attractive."

"Yeah, Ken Z," Estelle says.

"He walked up to me because he saw me reading Oscar Wilde, and he was reading one of his books too."

"What?" CaZZ exclaims.

Estelle can't believe her ears either. "He was reading Wilde?"

"This spring break affair is getting more and more interesting," CaZZ says.

"And I love it," Estelle says.

"What book?" CaZZ asks.

I tell them it was *De Profundis*. Their eyes widen with wonder.

"Tell us more," Estelle begs.

I tell them Ran was a huge fan of Oscar Wilde, knew a lot about his life. "He knew the name Oscar went by when he went to live in exile in Paris."

"Sebastian Melmoth," CaZZ says.

"Yes."

"It's fate, Ken Z," Estelle says. "You and he were destined to meet."

I shrug.

"So romantic," Estelle adds.

"So why is he so into Oscar Wilde?" CaZZ asks.

"Is he part of an Oscar Wilde book club?" Estelle asks.

"No," I reply.

"Too bad he doesn't go to our school," Estelle says. "He could be in our book club."

"Where does he live?" CaZZ asks.

I pause, then let out the news. "North Kristol."

I watch CaZZ's facial expression go from anticipation to disdain. I imagine it's the same reaction as mine when I first found out.

"So what was he doing in Mirage? Shopping?" CaZZ asks, a tinge of sarcasm in her voice.

"Killing time," I reply.

"Sure he was," CaZZ says.

"He was waiting for his mother, who works on thc base."

CaZZ nods, like people do when their suspicions are confirmed.

"Did you ever meet his mother?"

"No."

"Has he met yours?"

Again, no.

"And then what happened?" CaZZ asks.

Except for the parts I am not yet ready to share, I tell them the rest of the story, how he and I hung out every day of the break. How we saw each other a few more times after that, and then, before I knew it, he was gone.

"What do you mean 'he was gone'?"

"He disappeared," I reply.

"Disappeared?" CaZZ asks. "Or he stopped calling you?"

"He never called," I say, "only Zapped."

"When was his last Zap?"

"Couple weeks ago."

"But you continued to Zap him?"

"Countless times," I reply, editing the part about phoning Ran and getting that weird voice mail with the angry-sounding woman.

"Ken Z?"

"What?"

"What's Ran's last name?"

I shrug.

Silence.

Then I spell out what they're thinking. "I know." Pause. "He bunburyed me."

"It doesn't matter now, Ken Z," Estelle says, trying to comfort me.

"Maybe he did, Ken Z," CaZZ says. "But then again, maybe not. He's from the north, right? He probably can't do that over there. That's why he came here."

"To play with people's feelings," I say.

"Maybe," CaZZ says. "Or he came here to be himself."

"CaZZ is right, Ken Z," Estelle says.

"You ever go back to the mall?" CaZZ asks.

"Just once," I say. "Then I gave up."

Estelle gets a playful glint in her eye. "Got tired of waiting for the number eight?"

"Actually—yes," I say.

"If there's one thing to thank the bus from hell for, it's that it kills obsession fast," CaZZ says.

Suddenly, I feel something inside me rupturing.

Estelle notices it too. "Dude."

"Don't," I say, wincing. Too late. The moment her fingers graze my skin, something in me bursts. As if a blister that's been swelling up inside me these past weeks has finally been punctured, and all it took was the touch of a consoling friend. The next thing I know, I am sobbing with my head down, my whole body shaking, my chest heaving, my nose running.

Estelle throws her arms around me.

"Oh, sweetie," CaZZ says, rubbing my back.

"I . . . just want . . . him . . . you know . . . to come back . . . say bye." I try to push the words out between the heaving.

"I know, sweetie," CaZZ says. "I know." She reaches for her bag and passes me a tissue.

"As long as you were honest about your feelings, Ken Z, that's all that matters."

"I was," I say.

"We know," Estelle says.

Then, finally, it subsides. The sobbing, the shaking, the forcing of words. And what remain are silence and pure exhaustion. I feel like I just drained a sea of feelings from my body and all that's left for me to do is sleep.

"Sweetie, you okay?" CaZZ asks.

I nod.

"Dang, Ken Z, you look hot when you're breaking down," Estelle says. "You should fall in love more often."

"Whatever, Estelle," CaZZ says, rolling her eyes.

"Never again," I say.

"Never say never," CaZZ warns.

"But you've got to admit, Ken Z, it was incredible, right?" Estelle says.

"You mean Ran?" I ask. "Or the hurting?"

"I mean the four-letter word, dodo."

"Who made you the guru of love?" CaZZ asks.

"I fell too," Estelle says. "Twice."

"What?" CaZZ exclaims. "How come we don't know about them?"

"More details to come shortly," Estelle says, winking at me. "But it really is a four-letter word."

"Like *pain*," I say. "And *funk*."

"And *lies* and *mess*," CaZZ says.

"True," Estelle says.

"Ken Z?" CaZZ asks.

"That's not a four-letter word," I say, breaking the rhythm of our list.

"K-E-N-Z!" Estelle spells it out.

"H-U-R-T," I say.

"S-T-O-P," CaZZ says.

"H-E-A-L," Estelle says.

"W-H-E-N?" CaZZ asks.

"S-O-O-N," I say hesitantly.

"Soon?" CaZZ asks.

"Soon!" I say. This time, with an exclamation punch.

Lingering

Our last memory. Sunday night. We were in my room, standing face to face. He squinted; I squinted. I smiled; he smiled. We stood there, playing a game of mirrors. Until, gradually, silence reigned once more. He leaned his face close to mine. I could feel his warm breath flowing into my mouth, his lips almost touching mine. Then I withdrew. Because he withdrew. It wasn't a kiss he wanted after all, but to rest his head against my shoulder. I stood there, my arms folded around him, my hands in a tight clasp. I swayed. Because he swayed. Our bodies dancing to our own song. Then I stopped. Because he stopped. The two of us holding on to each other, lingering like a fading reverie. I could've stood there for another thousand and one minutes, savoring what would be our final embrace. Then he pulled away. He got very quiet. The expression on his face turned somber. I thought he was going to cry or say the inevitable. He did neither. He just stood there, looking at me, giving me the smile of history before surrendering his lips to mine.

FOR ESTELLE

In this world, no one
But you makes words so much fun
So gibbericious.

Splat

Sunday, 14 April. 2:47 a.m.

Can't sleep. My body is ready to splat but my mind is wide-awake. An hour ago, my mother came home from work. I was in bed, sitting up with my back to the wall, writing in my notebook. I didn't bother to shut the door or turn the light off. I didn't want her to think that I was asleep. No. Not to-night. I wanted her to peek in, say something, anything. She must've read the signs—bedroom light on, door wide open—because on her way to her room, she stopped in front of my door and knocked. "Ken Z . . ." She paused. I looked up and, for a moment, I wished I hadn't. She had this look on her face that didn't need me to explain why I was still up or why I was ditching school, neglecting my chores, keeping these nightly vigils.

She entered the room. "Here," she said, handing me more let-ters and packets from colleges and universities wanting to take part in shaping my future. I took the letters and placed them on the pile. She was about to leave when, suddenly, she turned around and stopped. She was about to say something but instead

just shook her head as if whatever she wanted to say didn't matter enough. But it would have.

Tonight, my frustration with silence from long ago returned to haunt me. I looked up at her. *Mom, please, say something, say anything to end these broken hours. I need your words tonight, Mom. No room for silence. Not with everything falling apart.*

"I am so lucky," she finally uttered. "So many worlds want you. They're all waiting for you, Ken Z. You and all your brightness. Just imagine the stories waiting to fill up your notebooks."

I smiled.

Because she smiled.

"Let this beginning be just that—one of the many stories."

Then, as quietly as she had entered my room, she walked away and left me with those good-night words that I will turn to during difficult nights like this.

Ken Z Uchida
Fifth Grade
Miss Amanda Buenaventura
Writing Assignment #5

Our Favorite Pastime

My mother loves to read. She reads all the time. She reads during the day and she reads late at night. She reads when she comes home from work even if she's tired. Sometimes she reads with the music on. Sometimes I hear her humming. Sometimes while she's reading she'll stop and look out, at nothing in particular, as if the book is taking her far, far away, like she's dreaming in another world. Someplace quiet and marvelous like Antarctica. I love to read too, especially in my room. With books I try on different worlds. I meet people who live inside stories. Stories I never want to end. That's when I know that I really like a book. I like endings the least. They make me sad, even when they end happily ever after. My mother is okay with endings, though. When she's done reading a book she returns it right away to the library, or donates it if it's hers. Then she goes and borrows or buys another book. I don't know how she does it, how she goes from one book to the next just like that. I don't know how anyone can do that. It's so easy for her. Not me. I have a hard time, especially if I love the characters and the story and the place too much. I reread the book. My mother said I have to learn to start practicing goodbyes to books or I won't have room for new stories. She's right. Still, it's hard even if all I'm doing is practicing goodbyes.

LIGHT

Live each word as if
The world depended on it—
Stay and read to me.

THE SILENCE LIST

There's the silence that drops from nowhere
And the silence that stabs like a shiny switchblade.

There's the silence that comes right at takeoff
And the kind that echoes long after a crash landing.

There's the silence that craves for attention
And the kind that aches to be left alone.

Silence like the red velvet curtain of an old theater
Full of history: thick and musty.

Silence confident as a period, breathless as a comma,
Endless as ellipses . . .

There's a silence lovers leave behind,
Like a suitcase on a platform after the last train.

There's a silence lovers arrive with,
Like a body crammed in a busload of strangers.

There's a silence waiting to breathe
And a silence crying to be broken.

There's a silence rare and breathtaking
As the time I caught her in her room,

Dancing with no music to guide her
Just a song playing loudly in her head

Leading her to another place,
Another her.

Away from here and away from her:
The woman with a thousand and one silences,

Who left behind a life in another country
So she did not have to answer to any man

Or walk five steps ahead of him
Or sleep with dreams bolted down.

This woman who made me see silence in words
And taught me how to shatter it

Whenever something was worth hearing.
My list of silence . . . my endless list: my mother.

The Memory of Paper

Monday, 15 April. 8:30 p.m.

Woke up this evening from a nap and found a brown packet right outside my door. Inside were seven bright-orange notebooks. Pocket-sized. Perfect for my lists, haikus, thought bubbles. I've always wanted to own one, but they're so pricey even my wish list can't afford them.

On the cover is DURABLE NOTES superimposed on a map of Antarctica. A slip of onionskin-thin paper is inserted between the pages; on it is a little story about the notebook. These notebooks, it says, are very popular among adventurers. In the past centuries, explorers used the same type of paper to record latitudes and longitudes. Geologists logged in seismic activities of volcanoes. Mountaineers sketched their hiking routes. Anthropologists and sociologists filled the pages with field notes. And writers and artists carry them around to store their dreams, memories, and ideas.

. . .

The paper is tear-resistant and is supposed to withstand the harshest weather conditions. In the last war, soldiers kept journals to describe the horrors of war and loneliness: what it was like to live with the memory of bombing villages, killing strangers, innocent women, and armed children. Many used them to write letters to their loved ones, or document their last will and testament. When the bodies of soldiers were returned to their families, these notebooks were found in the pockets of their jackets and pants.

Weatherproof. Futura typeface. And ellipses instead of ruled lines—those series of dots that mean infinity, that look like constellations connecting one small thought or feeling or dream to another and then another ad infinitum. As I am attempting this very moment.

The Visitation

MONDAY, 15 APRIL. EVENING. MY BEDROOM.

OSCAR: Get up, Ken Z!

ME: Oscar!

OSCAR: Enough of this darkness, Ken Z.

ME: No!

WITH ONE SWIFT MOTION, OSCAR DRAWS OPEN THE CURTAINS.
SUNLIGHT BARGES INTO THE ROOM LIKE AN INTRUDER.

OSCAR: No, Ken Z. Enough of this sadness. Wake up! Rise from
this recumbent posture.

ME: You're back!

OSCAR: I never left. Not completely.

ME: But I thought . . . You mean you're not mad?

OSCAR: Last I checked, dear boy, I wasn't the one firing the shots.

ME: Oh, Oscar, I'm so—

OSCAR: Never mind. It's a new day. Time to make a list.

ME: But all those hurtful words I hurled at you.

OSCAR: My dear child, your world was breaking. You had every
right to rage.

ME: I'm so sorry.

OSCAR: Hush; I gave you bad counsel; I apologize.

ME: No, no, no.

OSCAR: I only wanted you to experience what I thought would expand your universe.

ME: And it did, Oscar, it did. I swear. If only you can find it in your heart to forgive me, because I don't know if I can.

OSCAR: Don't be so unkind to yourself, Ken Z. You were merely loving. No one asks for his heart to be bruised. No one asks Love to take a detour, and as you well know, detours are also part of the adventure. There really is no way of telling Love's destination, Ken Z. It is that teacher that, like all brilliant teachers, always makes room for mistakes and memories, for growth and learning.

ME: I wouldn't have survived this adventure without you, Oscar. From the start of my hummingbird heartbeats. To my own . . .

OSCAR: . . . unraveling.

ME: Yes. Unraveling.

OSCAR: And what a privilege it is to be a spectator.

ME: But the play, I'm afraid is badly cast. Downsized now with the other lead missing.

OSCAR: It's a glorious spectacle, nonetheless.

ME: But you know you weren't just a spectator, Oscar. You were also a participant.

OSCAR: In the supporting role of the apparition, like the ghost of Hamlet's father.

JUST THEN, THE URGE TO CRY CREEPS UP.

OSCAR: Come now, dear heart. Hush.

ME *(wiping away the tears)*: Thank you, Oscar.

OSCAR: *Pourquoi?*

ME: For coming to my aid. For saving me. And others like me. You could not save yourself from Bosie, but you rescued me from my own drowning. And now, here you are once again, guiding me out of my gutter.

OSCAR: Gutter and stars. We've all been there, my dearest. Give it time. Brief or epic, it too will pass. Enjoy life, for life is short. Love, unfortunately, is even shorter. That's why I advised you to love spectacularly. Love with all its wonderment and endless flaws, its countless blessings and failures. Love for its devotion to rapture and forgiveness and uncertainty. There's so much to learn from such mystery. Endless, like your list.

ME: Like my list.

OSCAR: And, by the way, Ran is only a prelude.

ME: To this mystery?

OSCAR: Yes. Above all, dear boy, never lose that edge of yours. That edge to be yourself. Keep astonishing yourself. It is the only life worth living. Otherwise, it'll be impossible to love intensely, beautifully, and, in some places and cases, dangerously. For once it's over, you have the rest of the afterlife to be . . .

ME: . . . dusting?

OSCAR: Ah—yes. Dusting.

RAN

Tonight, I can write the saddest us.

To think once, under a giant moon,
you draped your arm across my shoulders.
It was so surreal I could not move,
gladly stuck between flight and surrender.

From you, I learned a random kind of happiness.
From you, I found another meaning to me.

Yet, tonight, when the blur in my world
no longer thrills me, I go to bed with you
tossing and turning in my thoughts,
my only wish to unlearn the kiss
and the craving that comes with it.

To see you one last time is all I'm asking for
so I can ask, Ran, was I ever a part
in your moments of happiness too?

Tonight, I can write the saddest us.
In the Book of Love, I liked you
and I think you liked me, too
inside our small universe where a billion
kinds of loneliness now reside.

A mislaid word is how I feel tonight.
You taught me comfort, Ran,

but forgot the part about my heart
and how to stop it
from unraveling.

Doubt is a certainty tonight
while your absence ransacks this room.

Tonight, I can write the saddest us.
Tonight, I can write the saddest us.

The Song of Broken Sleep

Tuesday, 16 April

It's almost two a.m., and the only reminder that I am still here,
broken sleep and all, is the sound of jazz playing softly in my
mother's bedroom. Miles Davis, Ella Fitzgerald, Billie Holiday,
Sarah Vaughn, John Coltrane, Anita O'Day. Jazz artists I have
grown to know and love listening to. They keep my mother company at night. There's Coltrane and his cool and sexy, sad sax.
There's Billie, who love-wails at the moon. Ella with her silk-
fine-and-mellow voice. Sarah and Anita, whose scats are like a
pack of wild cats chasing after a dream. Tonight, it's Chet Baker
on trumpet and vocals. In the thick silence of the night, I listen
to his voice crack as he sings about surrendering to memories,
like ghosts, that we thought we had forgotten or already made
peace with, memories that we never wanted and that continue
to punish us by making us crave and wish we were doing more
than just remembering.

The Muse This Time

TUESDAY, 16 APRIL. LATE NIGHT. MY BEDROOM.

OSCAR: Another masterpiece in the making, Ken Z?

ME: Nah. Just a haiku about my mother.

OSCAR: Ah—your muse this time! Mothers make great muses. My mother was my muse.

ME: What was she like?

OSCAR: She was a magnificent woman. An artist, a poet, and a revolutionary who fought for Ireland's independence. She ran a salon for Irish artists and writers. Without her, I don't think I would've become a writer. She gave me permission to follow my adventurous and rebellious nature. What about yours?

ME: She lives in her own little world.

OSCAR: Like Ken Z?

ME *(laughing)*: I guess you could say that. Parallel small worlds. She's the one who taught me how to read, and how to write haikus.

OSCAR: Ah! And your lists?

ME: From her too.

OSCAR: So she ushered you to the Gates of Imagination.

ME: Yes. I only wish she were a little more vocal.

OSCAR: What do you mean?

ME: She and I speak the language of silence.

OSCAR: Seventeen syllables?

ME: Or less. But, sometimes, I need to hear it, you know?

OSCAR: I understand.

ME: She means well. I know she does.

OSCAR: And where is she at this ungodly hour?

ME: She's supposed to be home now. Her shifts are long, sometimes thirteen, fourteen hours a day.

OSCAR: *Mon Dieu*, that's barely enough to make sleep worth dreaming about.

ME: She works a lot so she can send me to a good college. Far from here. That's what she wants.

OSCAR: And is this what you want?

ME: I don't want to leave her here by herself.

OSCAR: Is that the only reason?

ME: What do you mean?

OSCAR: Well, she was alone, you know, before you entered the picture.

ME: True.

OSCAR: Maybe you're afraid to take another risk and go outside your comfort zone.

ME: Maybe.

OSCAR: I wouldn't worry so much about that if I were you. If you can survive love, you can survive anything. As for your mother, mothers are stronger than we think. They are the scaffolds of our lives, Ken Z. They are there to protect us, to keep us from crumbling to pieces. It doesn't matter how far

we are, they are there, Ken Z, watching over us, shadowing us wherever we go, like memories. I think I hear her calling you. Adieu for now.

ME: Thanks, Oscar.

OSCAR: *De rien,* Monsieur Ken Z.

JAZZ

A gardenia
Behind her ear, my mother
Humming at the moon.

The Birth of a List

Restlessness keeps you up all night.
Make a list.
Morning wakes you up on the wrong side of the bed.
Make a list.

Make a list
Because it's root canal day
Because you bombed on the SAT, debate team,
cheerleading tryouts
Because you're broke, bored, beyond therapy
Because the bullies can't get enough of you.

Make a list
Because the boy of your dreams said "Yes!" to the prom
then, as you jumped for joy,
almost punching a hole in the ceiling,
he shouted, "April Fools'!"

Make a list
Why proms and homecoming dances are tacky, overrated,
and way overpriced.

Make a list
Why social media sucks and is for the insecure
born with narcissistic complexes.

Make a list
Because the party of your life has ghosted you
Because you're seesawing between hoping and breaking

Make a list
Because you're being such a dick to your friends
And they don't deserve it
Just as you don't deserve them.

Make a list because the elevator cable of your friendship
is about to snap.
HELP!!!

"Make a list, Ken Z,"
my mother says.
She's certain it'll save me.
The way it's saved her.

List compiler.
Jazz junkie.
Avid reader of haikus.
My mother, silent warrior from another time.
"This is who we are, Ken Z," she says.

List after list after list.
Where we've been, where we're going.
A million moments.

A million farewells.
A million questions.
The list keeps growing.
On to the next target.
The next memory.

"And when you're done," she says,
"make another.
Because a list is never finished.
It knows no limits.
Only possibilities."

Banned for Now

"I've got some bad news," Mr. Oku tells us. We knew something was up when he told me, CaZZ, Estelle, Matt, and Tanya to stay after class.

"Starting in September, when the new school year begins, I won't be allowed to teach Oscar Wilde anymore."

WTFs reverberated through the classroom.

"Unfortunately, his plays and *The Picture of Dorian Gray,* along with other books, are now banned," Mr. Oku continues.

"Banned?" Matt asks. "As in *forbidden*?"

Mr. Oku nods. "Of course, this new rule won't affect you, as you're all graduating next month."

Estelle is about to say something when Mr. Oku holds one hand up as he fills us in on what's been happening at school. Apparently, the banning of certain books has been on the agenda of the Department of Public Education, or DOPE. The government-appointed members of DOPE are in charge of designing class courses from kindergarten to twelfth grade. They are the ones who come up with the reading lists.

295

A group of educators, including Mr. Oku, had been fighting hard to oppose it and, for some time, had been successful in blocking it. But early this week, DOPE unanimously voted to change the curriculum. The three most affected courses are history, journalism (which handles the bimonthly school paper), and literature.

"So what books are they banning?" Tanya asks.

"Probably *1984*," Matt says. *1984* was one of the first novels we read in Mr. Oku's class. Set in a society that's under constant surveillance by Big Brother, it made me think a lot about our own world riddled with wars, terrorist attacks, and lives controlled by a government-monitored technology.

"It's probably too freaky and eerie for DOPE minds," Estelle says.

"Too close to home," I say.

"Because it *is* home," CaZZ says. "North Kristol as Big Brother."

"Those surveillance cameras are on practically every block now," Tanya adds. "Plus our letters and packages have to go through their Customs first. I cannot even order panties online without my privacy getting invaded."

"I'm sure that's not the only thing they know about you," CaZZ says. "They probably have trolls reading our emails and chats and going through our browsing history."

"They probably control what we can and cannot access on the Web," I say. "Mr. Oku, didn't you move here because you weren't allowed to teach Oscar Wilde in North Kristol?"

"That's right," Mr. Oku answers.

"Well, I tried doing a search on 'Oscar Wilde and North Kristol' and came up with nothing," I say. "Same when I tried searching for 'banned books in North Kristol.'"

"Because they don't want you to know that their shit stinks," CaZZ says.

"Are these the reasons why they're banning *1984*, Mr. Oku?" Matt probes.

Shaking his head, Mr. Oku takes a sheet of paper from his folder and reads from it. "According to DOPE, Orwell's *1984* is banned because 'the novel promotes an atmosphere of fear, paranoia, sex, and violence.'"

"What about their reasons for banning Oscar Wilde?" Tanya asks.

"Hello?" CaZZ says. "*The Picture of Dorian Gray* has underground opium dens, suicide, murder, and closeted homosexuals."

"It reeks of homoerotic undertones," Matt says.

"That's an understatement," CaZZ says.

Reading from the report again, Mr. Oku says, "'Satanic in nature, *The Picture of Dorian Gray* tempts individuals to lead a life of vices, of immorality that culminates in self-destruction.'"

"But 'there is no such thing as a moral or an immoral book,'" Matt says, quoting one of the famous lines from *The Picture of Dorian Gray*. "'Books are either well, or badly, written.'"

"Good job, Matt," CaZZ says, winking at him.

"What about *The Importance of Being*—" Before I can finish, Mr. Oku is already nodding, saying, "All of Oscar Wilde's plays are banned."

"Why? For promoting dandyism?" Tanya asks.

"No," Estelle says, "for promoting identity crises."

"'Oscar Wilde's plays promote identity theft and the art of deception,'" Mr. Oku reads from the paper.

"Bunburying!" Tanya exclaims.

"Correct," Mr. Oku says.

For a moment, the mention of bunburying winds my memory back to my and Ran's very beginning at Mirage.

Matt disagrees. "But Oscar's plays are comedies," he says. "They're witty and ironic. And no one gets hurt by the deception."

"Apparently, Oscar's wit and irony weren't enough to convince the brilliant minds of DOPE," Mr. Oku says.

"What a bunch of bullshit!" CaZZ exclaims. "They're banning Oscar Wilde because he was capital G-A-Y."

"I thought he was bi," Matt says.

CaZZ rolls her eyes. "Tack on whatever label you want, Matt. But the truth, plain and simple, was that he was arrested and charged and wrongfully indicted without hard evidence to prove the allegations."

"True that," Tanya says.

"I don't understand," Matt says. "Why should Oscar Wilde's sexuality be an issue when it's not a crime here in South Kristol to be gay?"

We all turn to Matt, flabbergasted by his asinine remark. Has he forgotten the ordeal CaZZ lived through?

"Ever watch the news lately, Matt," Estelle snaps, "with all the bullying and bashing and high suicide rate among teens, and not a single law or shelter to protect us?"

Matt falls silent, hangs his head in shame.

"I'm sorry, CaZZ," Matt says. "Forgive me."

"It's okay, Matt," CaZZ says, sincerity in her voice.

"Mr. Oku," Tanya says, "are the Harry Potter books banned too?"

"Third on the list," Mr. Oku replies.

"What the—"

"For promoting dark arts?" Matt says, half-joking.

" 'For advocating reading as magical thinking,' " Mr. Oku says.

"Seriously?" CaZZ asks.

"In fine print." Mr. Oku holds up the report.

"So we're not even supposed to use our imagination anymore?" CaZZ asks.

"Death to the imagination!" Estelle exclaims. "Viva Aurora Boring Alice!"

"What about Judy Blume's *Forever*?" Tanya asks.

"Hello? That's so '70s teen porn," CaZZ says.

" 'Blume's *Forever* promotes sex, promiscuity, and Planned Parenthood,' " Mr. Oku says.

"So if *Forever* is banned, does that mean Charlotte Madison's books are banned too?" CaZZ asks, referring to the overhyped vampire trilogy.

"I couldn't get past chapter one of *Jupiter Rising*," Tanya says.

"Me neither," I say.

"*Vernal Equinox* tried too hard to be kinky with vampires trying to out-neck each other," Estelle remarks.

"*Mercury Retrograde* was a total letdown," Matt says about the last book in the trilogy.

"I hate to disappoint you," Mr. Oku says, "but Charlotte Madison's books are not on the list."

"Of course not," CaZZ retorts. "Those books promote abstinence. The vampires died if they had premarital sex."

"Imagine being a four-hundred-year-old virgin," Tanya says. "All wrinkled up like a sun-dried tomato."

"What about *The Catcher in the Rye*?" I ask, about the coming-of-age novel about a beautiful loser written by a boozed-up loner.

"J. D. Salinger's novel is first on the list," Mr. Oku says.

"But I heart Holden Caulfield," Tanya says of the main character. "I didn't finish it, but he's someone I can imagine dating."

"No wonder it's banned," Matt jokes.

Everyone laughs, including Mr. Oku.

"DOPE probably read it as a manual for losers," I say.

"And it contains profanity," Estelle adds.

"Here's what DOPE had to say," Mr. Oku says. "'*The Catcher in the Rye* promotes antisocial behavior and inspires youths to be high school dropouts and renegades.'"

"This is really sad, Mr. Oku," I say, remembering how much we had loved the novel in class. It was depressing, but Holden's confusion and loneliness, even though he came from a privileged background, hit home for many of us.

"It is sad, Ken Z," Mr. Oku says.

"Holden was like the friend we could've saved," CaZZ says.

"But perhaps DOPE sees Holden as a bad influence instead of a troubled teen," Mr. Oku says.

"So instead they want us to read books we can't relate to," CaZZ says, which means the less we connect with the stories, the better.

"Reading about vampire virgins is safer," I say.

"Imagine when it's your books, Ken Z," CaZZ says. "Books about us, our experiences, our stories, our memories, our histories, this place—South Kristol."

"They'll probably get banned before the others," Estelle says.

"Why do you say that?" Mr. Oku asks.

"Because how dare we write our own stories, in our own voices?" CaZZ answers.

"True that," Tanya says.

"Banning our books would be their way of erasing us, of making us—and the world we live in—invisible," CaZZ says.

"Pretty soon, they're going to make us believe Robinson Crusoe was stranded on an island without natives living there," Matt says.

"Or Huck Finn crossed the Mississippi River without Jim," Estelle says.

"They don't want us to read about our side of the truth," I continue.

"You tell it, Ken Z," Tanya says.

"So what's going to happen to the Earnest Book Club?" I ask. "Is this it? After us, no more Oscar Wilde?"

"That's the other reason for this meeting," Mr. Oku says. "Apparently, Principal Deedy found out about our book club."

Tanya turns to Matt.

Matt immediately reacts. "Why look at me?"

Tanya steadies her glare on him.

"I would never snitch," Matt says. "I promise to God."

"I believe you, Matt," Estelle says.

"Thanks."

"I don't think it came from any of you," Mr. Oku says. "And that's what we have to keep in mind. Pointing fingers won't get

us anywhere. We have to stick up for each other more so now than before."

"So what did Principal Deedy say?" Matt asks.

"We're no longer permitted to use the classroom to hold our meetings," Mr. Oku says.

"That's the stupidest thing I ever heard," Tanya says.

"You mean to tell us, Mr. Oku, that it's okay for church people to use our campus every weekend? But God forbid if we use our own classroom to talk about *books* once a month?" Estelle asks.

"Apparently so," Mr. Oku says.

"What if we meet off campus?" I suggest. "Can they still ban us?"

"Absolutely not. They can ban us teachers from assigning Oscar's books in class. But outside of school, they cannot stop me, you, or any of us from reading them."

"Then good," CaZZ says, "because Allan Isaac and his LGBTQ posse want to continue the Earnest Book Club next year."

"Aren't you afraid, Mr. Oku?" Matt asks. "What if you get in trouble?"

Mr. Oku shakes his head. "Absolutely not. They can ban it in school, but there isn't a law in South Kristol against having an Oscar Wilde book club."

"Not yet, anyway," CaZZ says.

"Gee, I didn't know reading could be this dangerous," Tanya remarks.

"Reading is only dangerous to those who are afraid to imagine," Mr. Oku says. "If there is one thing I hope you got out of the Earnest Book Club, it is that each of you is not afraid to use your imagination. That you have accepted Oscar Wilde's invita-

tion to dare. The dare to read books, banned or not. The dare to think. The dare to imagine. The dare to speak your mind. And the dare to be yourself."

"Viva the Earnest Book Club!" Estelle shouts.

"Viva Oscar Wilde!" Tanya yells.

"Viva us!" CaZZ roars.

LAST RITES

Surrounded by books
Oscar Wilde spent his last hours
Dying and reading.

THE OUTCAST LIST

I'm a labyrinth of I's.
A winding staircase of whys.
A wall of doubts.
A sea of uncertainties.
A walking excess emotional baggage.
A dust in progress,
like our prom king and queen,
though they don't want me
in their Palace of Acceptance.
It's fine.
Belonging is overrated anyway,
and overcrowded.
I'm happy being the Emperor
of Loners and Library Loiterers.
Plus I'm a proud member
of a Wilde-worshiping club
that also stars a born-again jock,
a gender blurrer,
a cheerleader at the bottom of a pyramid,
and a girl warrior.
Fierce and fine.
We're queer that way.
Very Wildean that way.

CAZZ'S ADVICE TO OUTCASTS, YOUNG AND OLD

Howl back like the winds
Embrace the storm that you are—
Love, Hurricane CaZZ

Thursday-Morning Memento

THURSDAY, 18 APRIL. MORNING. MY BEDROOM.

ME: Great. Just great.

OSCAR: What's the matter?

ME: It's Elroy. He's missing.

OSCAR: Elroy?

ME: My emperor penguin paperweight. It's gone.

OSCAR: Oh dear. Where did you last see it?

ME: Right here. On my desk. Where it should be. *(Sighing)* Ran always played with it whenever he came over. He'd toss it in the air, then catch it with his palm.

OSCAR: Aha.

ME: What?

OSCAR: Could it be . . . ?

ME: You don't think he . . . ?

OSCAR: Well . . .

ME: What would he do with it? It's got a chipped flipper.

OSCAR: The more special.

ME: But why would he take my broken penguin? To spite me further? Was breaking my heart not enough?

OSCAR: Memento, my dear Ken Z. Memento.

ME: To remember me? For what?

OSCAR: Because, Ken Z, you're a rarity. Emperor extraordinaire.

Coda

One of the few things I learned from voice lessons (See False-Start List) is the coda. Its symbol is a cross over an *O,* like what a sniper sees through the scope of his rifle when he's aiming at a target. In the world of music, it is an extended passage that concludes the piece; it makes the composition whole. Mr. Harris, my former band teacher, likened it to an afterthought, sort of like the PS in a letter. But a very important one, for it gives an ending, a closure, to a musical journey. Quickiepedia describes it best, as "an addition that ends a piece or a movement." Tonight feels very much like that. A coda.

We are in my room. CaZZ, Estelle, and me. The Three Musketeers, Little Pigs, Blind Mice, Stooges, Amigos. CaZZ said they were in the neighborhood and decided to surprise me. I don't buy it; I know them better. They know it too. They're here for two reasons: (1) to make sure I didn't have a relapse and end up back in the gutter, and (2) to know more about the evolution of my romance. It's their way of

309

feasting on my love and, at the same time, getting me to let the pain out.

Estelle's approach is more subtle, playful. But CaZZ's tactic is asking frank questions that force me to face facts.

"Ken Z, were you two ever an official couple?"

I mull over her question.

The closest Ran and I got to being officially us
was him asking me:
"Ken Z, want to be random with me?"

The closest I got was "Yes."

I shake my head. No, it wasn't official, unless I count the time he confessed to me that he wished *it* had begun the way *ours* did. And though I did not ask him what he meant by IT, I had an inkling that IT was another love, from another time, with another guy—or girl. I did not want to open that can of worms, so I'd glossed over it.

"What difference does it make, CaZZ?" Estelle asks, sounding a bit irritated. "Official or not, it was love."

"I'm sorry, Ken Z. I didn't mean to offend," CaZZ says. "I only wanted to hear about the romance and it came out the wrong way. I know you're heartbroken, but I'm glad you experienced it."

"Yeah, Ken Z, you were in such a daze," Estelle says, "you were walking past cloud nine."

"Was I that obvious?" I ask.

They both nod. "We knew something wonderful was up," CaZZ says.

"Hello?" Estelle says. "You gelled your hair."

"You were so damn cute, so charming," CaZZ continues.

"You were vervacious. You were Ken Zing," Estelle says, complimenting me with two words from her *Dictionary of Made-Up Words.*

"You had on a smile we had never seen before," CaZZ says.

I roll my eyes. "Well, so much for that."

They detect my sarcasm. I fall silent. I can feel the heavy sinking feeling coming on, but it doesn't linger.

"Ran might be the most unwanted person on your list right now, Ken Z," CaZZ says, "but if there's one awesome thing that he did, it's that he changed your world."

CaZZ's remarks make me think of Ran's last Zap.

313

Estelle jumps in and says, "She's right, Ken Z. But you also changed his."

"Not enough," I say. "Or he wouldn't have pulled a Houdini."

"Maybe it was getting too much for him and he got scared," CaZZ says.

"I was scared too," I say. "We could've been scared together."

"Synchronized scaredy-cats," Estelle says, laughing, then: "Sorry, I couldn't help myself."

I laugh because CaZZ does.

Then she sobers up. "Maybe his mother found out."

"Let's not waste time on maybes," Estelle says.

"She's right," CaZZ says. "Just one more question. What's your last memory of him?"

Another question to mull over. I rewind time to that last night. I can see the two of us in my room, standing, embracing, holding on to each other's stillness. I open my mouth, but the memory has me by the throat. The first word cracks in my voice. I can feel my eyes tearing up. The memory is too raw; the wound is still healing.

Estelle senses my discomfort. From the corner of my eye, I see her sending a signal to CaZZ. "Detour, CaZZ, detour."

"It can wait, Ken Z," CaZZ says.

"Yeah, Ken Z," Estelle says, winking. "Share it when you're good and ready."

"So what do I do now?" I ask.

"Well, going to North Kristol is definitely out of the question," CaZZ says. "Too many red flags. Too expensive."

"Too risky," Estelle says. "Plus you don't know where he lives."

"You might end up getting interrogated," CaZZ says. "They'll want to know who you're looking for and why."

"It will only double the trouble," Estelle concludes.

"I guess I have no choice but to start all over," I say.

"No, Ken Z," CaZZ says, "you keep going forward. You have your notebooks, your haikus, your lists. At least he didn't take those away."

"Yeah, at least Ran didn't pull a Bosie on you," Estelle says.

"Because you didn't let him," CaZZ says.

I nod. They're right. At least Ran did not take me away from my notebooks. I still wrote when I could. I wrote because I wanted to save everything.

"Can you imagine if Ran got in the way of your haikus?" CaZZ asks.

"I'd go to North Kristol and hunt him down myself," Estelle says.

"Me too," CaZZ says.

"What you need is closure-foreclosure, Ken Z," Estelle says.

"I agree," CaZZ says.

"How?" I ask.

The three of us fall silent. Then the answer hit us all at once.

"Hello?" Estelle says, overlapping with CaZZ's "A list!"

"It's not that easy."

"Of course it is, Ken Z," Estelle says. "You're the Jedi Master of lists."

"May the list be with you," CaZZ says.

She and Estelle laugh.

Because I laughed.

SENT MONDAY 3/18, 2:23 A.M.

Ken Z—
"The world is changed
because you are made of ivory
and gold. The curves
of your lips rewrite history."

ALMOST

Almost heart.
Almost dear.
Almost us.
Almost done.
Almost scar.
Almost sigh.
Almost there.

THE HOW-TO-DEAL-WITH-A-BROKEN-HEART LIST

Take up yoga.

Bang my head until I reach nirvana.

Avoid watching romantic comedies, they always end happily.

Avoid watching romantic dramas; they always end in death.

Start a support group for ghosting victims.

Avoid musicals, especially with dying teens in them.

Make an anime tracing the evolution of my stupidity.

Upload my pain on U-Tube.

Work on perfecting my OCD skills.

Count the number of dots inside an impressionist painting.

Upgrade my suffering: study the mourning rituals of gorillas.

Avoid sci-fi flicks, especially with dying teens killing each other.

Stick to horror and cooking and home repair shows.

Pack up for Antarctica.

Get a second, third, fourth opinion on me.

Stay in corpse pose forever.

The Problem with Good and Bye

What am I supposed to do with all these wonderful feelings and memories mixed in with the not-so-wonderful? I'm stuck. And Ran is no help. I'm not sure he'll ever reappear. I'm not counting on it.

So if he's crossed me out of his life, does this mean I have to do the goodbye thing all by myself? Is that even possible? Don't you need two people for a goodbye to work? One says it while the other, who will agree or not, listens. Two. Just like its total number of words.

"Good." As in "Good riddance, Ken Z!"

And.

"Bye." As in "No!"

So how can I bid him goodbye when he is not here to say it is or isn't so?

Specifics

When I was small, my mother used to teach me Japanese words. One of the things she told me was never to use the popular *sayonara* when bidding goodbye, especially to her or anyone I loved. I forgot why but her warning stuck with me. I never got around to asking her. Maybe it's because I never needed to. Until tonight.

On her way to her room, I stop to ask her what the other word for "goodbye" is in Japanese, other than *sayonara*.

"There are many," she replies. "It depends on who's saying it."

"What do you mean?"

"There's a 'goodbye' for the one who's leaving."

"Which is?"

"*Ittekimasu.*" She spells the word as I jot it down in my notebook. "But that's a goodbye that means 'I'll be right back.' And the person he's talking to will reply *'itterasshai'* or *'ki o tsukete,'* which are goodbyes that mean 'Please go and come back' and 'Take care.'"

Fascinating how specific the Japanese are about their goodbyes. It reminds me of the Inuits and their different words for snow. I guess there are different ways of falling, as there are different ways of parting.

"What about *sayonara*?" I ask. "I remember you telling me never to use that word."

"Japanese people seldom use it. Not unless they mean it."

"Then how come it's so popular?"

She shrugs. "Maybe Americans never bothered to learn the other goodbyes because there are just too many or they were too lazy to remember. Or maybe it's the only goodbye the Japanese taught the Americans when they occupied Japan during the war."

"Why? What does *sayonara* mean?"

"You only say that when you're not going to see the person for a very, very long time." She pauses before adding, "Perhaps never."

"As in goodbye forever?"

She nods.

I imagine gazillions of people bidding each other *sayonara* without knowing what it really means.

I look up to find her smiling at me faintly, a tinge of sadness in her eyes.

I smile back to let her know I'll be all right. "*Domo arigato,* Ma," I say, thanking her in her native language.

She welcomes me with "*Do ittashimaste,*" then "*Oyasuminasai,* Ken Z."

"Good night to you too, Ma."

As she's about to close the door, she says, "Make a list, Ken Z," which, to her, holds different meanings. Tonight, it means "recharge."

"I will, Ma," I say. "I will."

"Sayonara, Ken Z. . . ."

"Sayonara, Ran."

HEART

Learn from the clouds.
Promising nothing—
Even rain.

There are two ways to end this story.

There are two ways to end this story.

The first is a haiku.

REBEL LOVE

Dear Divine Oscar,
Yes, we are the dare in love.
Yours truly, Ken Z.

The second is a kiss sealed with a list.

THE BEAUTIFUL THINGS LIST

Getting lost inside the mind of a list.

My bedroom window, rain-draped.

A garden of gardenias for my mother.

Skipping-stone words.

Serendipity.

Perspicacity.

Forsythia.

Water-lily-in-a-drinking-glass moment.

Imagination on full blast.

Autumn leaves in ink on paper.

CaZZ as Dorian Gray, in a velvet waistcoat, breeches, and cloak.

*Estelle rebelling in a winter prom gown with spaghetti
  straps and knee-high black leather combat boots.*

Me looking wild in tux, top hat, and ivory cane.

Bling it on.

*The verb "to remember" in Spanish—recordar—means
  "to pass back through the heart."*

Concentric circles on a pond.

*Salmon risking everything to see their birthplace perhaps
  for the last time.*

*A male penguin battling an Antarctic storm with an egg
  nestled between his legs.*

Jocks passionately (mis)quoting Oscar Wilde.

Eternity in one moment.

*My mother lost and mellow while listening to Duke
  Ellington's "Daydream."*

The saga of a kiss.

The sigh that completes it.

The world shut its gateway against me,
but the door of Love remains open.

—OSCAR WILDE

Chronology

1854

October 16. Oscar Fingal O'Flahertie Wills Wilde is born in Dublin, Ireland. His father, Sir William Wilde, is an eye and ear doctor and a writer. His mother, Jane Francesca Elgee Wilde, an Irish nationalist, is also a poet. Oscar has two siblings: an elder brother, William Charles Kingsbury (born 1852) and a younger sister, Isola Emily Francesca (born 1857).

1864–1871

Oscar attends Portora Royal School, a boarding school at Enniskillen.

1867

Isola dies of a fever. She is only nine years old.

1871

Oscar is awarded a Royal School scholarship to Trinity College, Dublin, where he studies classics.

1874

Oscar earns a scholarship to study at Magdalen College in Oxford. Oscar is twenty years old. During this period, he begins to attract attention and criticism for his eccentric and dandyesque taste in clothes (e.g., velvet cloaks and capes, knee breeches, fur-collared coats).

1876

Oscar's father dies.

1878

Oscar wins the Newdigate Prize for his poem "Ravenna." The annual award is given to an Oxford undergraduate for best poem.

1879

Oscar graduates from Oxford with honors in classics and moves to London.

1881

Oscar publishes his first book of poetry, titled simply *Poems.*

1882

Oscar travels to the United States to lecture on aesthetics. His first play, *Vera; or, the Nihilists* premieres unsuccessfully in New York.

1883

Oscar's second play, *The Duchess of Padua,* is staged in London. It is also unsuccessful.

1884

Oscar marries Constance Lloyd, the wealthy daughter of a Dublin barrister. The newlyweds move to a house on Tite Street, in the artistic neighborhood of Chelsea.

1885

Oscar and Constance's first child, Cyril, is born.

The Criminal Law Amendment Act is passed. Under section 11, homosexuals could be imprisoned for up to two years of hard labor if found guilty of gross indecency. No hard evidence was needed; testimony was sufficient. Homosexuality will not be decriminalized in England until 1967, seventy-two years after the trial of Oscar Wilde.

1886

Vyvyan, the couple's second son, is born.

1887

Oscar takes over as editor of the *Woman's World;* he works there for two years. He also meets Robert "Robbie" Ross, who will go on to become one of his best friends and, later, his literary executor.

1888

Oscar publishes *The Happy Prince and Other Tales,* his first collection of fairy tales.

1889

Oscar publishes several essays, including "The Decay of Lying."

1891

Oscar publishes several essays and books, including two collections of short stories, *Lord Arthur Savile's Crime* and *A House of Pomegranates,* and his only novel, *The Picture of Dorian Gray,* which was serialized in *Lippincott's Monthly Magazine* in 1890. The novel puts Oscar at the center of a controversy. Straitlaced Victorian critics attacked it for its immorality and homoerotic overtones.

Oscar meets Lord Alfred Douglas, aka "Bosie."

Oscar is commissioned by George Alexander to write a play. Begins working on his third play, *Lady Windermere's Fan.*

1892

Lady Windermere's Fan premieres at the St. James's Theatre in London. It is an instant hit. Writes *Salomé,* his first play in French. It is immediately banned because of a law in England that forbids the staging of plays featuring biblical characters.

Oscar begins writing *A Woman of No Importance.*

1893

A Woman of No Importance opens to critical and commercial success.

Oscar begins work on another play, *An Ideal Husband.*

1894

Oscar begins writing *The Importance of Being Earnest.*

1895

Oscar is at the height of his career, with two new plays premiering simultaneously in London—*An Ideal Husband* at Haymarket Theater and *The Importance of Being Earnest* at the St. James's Theatre. Both plays are commercial and critical hits.

February 18. The Marquess of Queensberry, Bosie's father, leaves a calling card for Wilde at the posh Albemarle Club. On it is the infamous inscription *For Oscar Wilde posing as a Somdomite.* Oscar sues Bosie's father for libel.

April 3. The libel trial *Oscar Wilde v. the Marquess of Queensberry* begins. Oscar's suit rebounds on him.

April 6. Queensberry is acquitted. Oscar is immediately arrested on charges of gross indecency. That evening, gay men, fearing persecution, flee England for Paris.

April 26. The trial of *Oscar Wilde v. the Crown* begins. Bosie leaves London for France. Oscar's wife, Constance, takes their sons to Europe. She changes their last name to Holland. Oscar never sees his boys again.

May 1. The case ends with a mistrial. Oscar is released on bail.

May 20. A third trial is set in motion.

May 27. Oscar is found guilty of gross indecency and sentenced to two years of imprisonment with hard labor. Imprisoned at Pentonville.

July 4. Transferred to Wandsworth Prison.

November 20. Transferred to Reading Gaol, where he will serve his remaining sentence.

1896

Oscar's mother dies. Oscar is not allowed to attend the funeral, nor was his mother allowed to visit him during his incarceration.

1897

Oscar writes *De Profundis*. Released from prison, he travels to France, where he spends the remaining years of his life in exile under the alias Sebastian Melmoth.

Oscar and Bosie reunite in Rouen, France, then take up residence near Naples, Italy. Their reunion experiences a brief bliss before it sours. They separate and Oscar moves into the Hôtel d'Alsace on rue des Beaux Arts in Paris.

1898

Oscar publishes "The Ballad of Reading Gaol," his most quoted and popular poem. Based on a factual account about a soldier who is sentenced to death for murdering his wife.

Oscar's wife dies in Italy. She is forty years old.

1900

November 30. Oscar Wilde dies of cerebral meningitis at the Hôtel d'Alsace. He is forty-six. He is first interred in the Cimetière de Bagneaux. In 1909, his remains are transferred to the Cimetière du Père Lachaise.

Bibliography

The following bibliography is a list of books by or about Oscar Wilde that inspired and guided me throughout this project. Some of his lines in the novel I borrowed from his plays, stories, and letters. My gratitude to the biographers, editors, and writers of the following books:

Ellmann, Richard. *Oscar Wilde*. Vintage, New York, 1988.

Fryer, Jonathan. *Robbie Ross: Oscar Wilde's Devoted Friend*. Carroll & Graf, New York, 2002.

Holland, Merlin. *The Complete Letters of Oscar Wilde*. Henry Holt, New York, 2000.

Holland, Merlin, ed. *The Real Trial of Oscar Wilde*. Harper Perennial, New York, 2004.

Holland, Merlin. *The Wilde Album*. Henry Holt and Company, New York, 1997.

Hyde, Montgomery H. *Oscar Wilde*. Da Capo Press, New York, 1981.

Kaufman, Moises. *Gross Indecency: The Three Trials of Oscar Wilde*. Vintage, New York, 1998.

Pritchard, David. *The Irish Biographies: Oscar Wilde*. Geddes & Grosset, Scotland, 2001.

Redman, Alvin, ed. *The Wit and Humor of Oscar Wilde*. Dover, New York, 1959.

Schmidgall, Gary. *The Stranger Wilde*. Plume Penguin, New York, 1994.

Wilde, Oscar. *The Complete Works of Oscar Wilde*. Harper & Row, New York, 1989.

Extremely Grateful Acknowledgments

This book would not have happened if not for the endless support, encouragement, and friendship of the following amazing people. Thank you to:

Kirby Kim, überagent, for introducing me to Kate Sullivan, who saw the possibilities for this book and took me there. Mahalo nui loa, Kate, for being so patient with me, several years of back-and-forth editing and the wonderful surprises that came with them. Thank you, too, Alexandra Hightower, for your enthusiasm and keen insights; they gave me additional fuel during the revision process.

To Shawn Mizukani, Shelley Nishimura, Shirley Abe, Lucy Purcell, and Jaymee T. Siao: my readers who believed in, and loved, Ken Z so much they cheered me on even when I was running on low-bat or losing interest.

To Gabriela Diccion Ocreto. I could not have asked for a better young adult reader and critic. Your instant feedback blew me away.

To Brenna English-Loeb and folks at Janklow & Nesbit Associates.

To Allan Isaac, Jeffrey Rebudal, Marco A. V. Lopez, David

Blackmore, Marissa Diccion Ocreto, and Mike Santos: thank you for offering me your homes when I needed a break.

To Katrina Tuvera, Paolo Manalo, and Rudy Quimbo, for the memorable dinner with unending wit and laughter.

To Faye Kicknosway, Lois-Ann Yamanaka, Lisa Asagi, Lori Takayesu, and Justin Chin (in memoriam).

To Jessica Hagedorn, Karen Tei Yamashita, Lucy Burns, Anjali Arondekar, Robert Diaz, Christine Balance, Martin Manalansan, and Meredith Nichols.

To Gordon Wong and Bill Maliglig: thank you for the magic room, my refueling station. And to Marlene Chong for listening.

To Macdowell Colony, where the final revision began and ended. Thank you for creating such a sanctuary for artists. And in memory of Ernest and Red Heller who funded my 8-week residency there.

To my family and friends in the U.S. and the Philippines.

And last, but certainly far from the least, muchas gracias con mil besitos to Oscar Wilde, for without your wit and heartbreak, Ken Z and I would be so lost.

About the Author

Poet, novelist, and playwright **R. Zamora Linmark** was born in Manila and educated in Honolulu. He is the author of four poetry collections and the novels *Leche* and *Rolling the R's*, which he's adapted for the stage. He currently resides in Honolulu and Manila.